"Are you rea̶̶̶ ̶̶̶ ̶̶̶ ̶̶̶ ̶̶̶ ̶̶̶ ̶̶̶ without ever̶ ̶̶̶ ̶̶̶ ̶̶̶ ̶̶̶ ̶̶̶ the time to look at it? It's a beautiful place."

"I'm sure it is, but I have no need of a ranch, dude ranch or otherwise."

"I think you're making a mistake, Cash."

Cash lifted a brow. At any other time, he didn't care what any person, man or woman, thought about any decision he made, but for some reason what Brianna thought mattered.

It shouldn't.

What he should do was thank her for joining him for lunch, and even tell her she did not have to join him on the walk back. In other words, he should put as much distance between them as possible.

He couldn't.

* * *

The Marriage He Demands by Brenda Jackson
is part of the Westmoreland Legacy:
The Outlaws series.

BRENDA JACKSON

THE MARRIAGE HE DEMANDS

HARLEQUIN
DESIRE

Recycling programs
for this product may
not exist in your area.

ISBN-13: 978-1-335-23282-3

The Marriage He Demands

Harlequin Enterprises ULC
22 Adelaide St. West, 40th Floor
Toronto, Ontario M5H 4E3, Canada
www.Harlequin.com

Printed in U.S.A.

Brenda Jackson is a *New York Times* bestselling author of more than one hundred romance titles. Brenda lives in Jacksonville, Florida, and divides her time between family, writing and traveling. Email Brenda at authorbrendajackson@gmail.com or visit her on her website at brendajackson.net.

Books by Brenda Jackson

Harlequin Desire

The Westmoreland Legacy

The Rancher Returns
His Secret Son
An Honorable Seduction
His to Claim
Duty or Desire

Westmoreland Legacy: The Outlaws

The Wife He Needs
The Marriage He Demands

Visit her Author Profile page at Harlequin.com, or brendajackson.net, for more titles.

You can also find Brenda Jackson on Facebook, along with other Harlequin Desire authors, at Facebook.com/harlequindesireauthors!

To the man who will always and forever be
the love of my life, Gerald Jackson Sr.

Therefore shall a man leave his father and
his mother, and shall cleave unto his wife:
and they shall be one flesh.
—*Genesis* 2:24

One

"What's wrong, Cash?"

Cashen Outlaw eased down into the chair in front of his brother Garth's desk. He then said the words he'd never thought about saying. "Bart just called. He got word that Ellen has died."

Garth Outlaw leaned forward in his chair as he studied his brother. "I'm sorry to hear that, Cash."

Cash nodded, at the moment not able to reply. Their father, Bart, had been married five times. Each of his sons had a different mother. Ellen had been Bart's third wife, and Cash's mother. Like the two wives before her and the two after, Bart had managed to divorce Ellen and get full custody of any child born to their union.

Cash didn't really recall his mother. He still had a picture of her tucked away that had yellowed with age. She was the only one of the five wives who'd called Bart's bluff and took him to court for custody of their son. She lost the battle and was never heard from again. Over the years, Cash hadn't received even a telephone call, birthday card or holiday greeting. It was as if she'd dropped off the face of the earth.

He had often thought about finding her, but didn't want to risk the pain of rejection like Garth had felt when he'd found his mother. Over the years Cash had decided that if his mother ever wanted to see him, she knew where he was. He and his family still lived in Fairbanks, Alaska, where their multimillion-dollar company, Outlaw Freight Lines, was located.

"When is the funeral, so the four of us can be there for you? I'll let Sloan, Maverick and Jess know. Charm won't be returning from Australia until next month."

Twenty-five-year-old Charm was their only sister and the youngest of all Bart's offspring. To this day, Charm's mother, Claudia, was the only woman Bart had ever loved, and she'd been the only one Bart had not married...but not for lack of trying.

"No need. Ellen didn't want a memorial service, and there won't be a funeral either. According to the information Bart received, Ellen wanted her body donated to science. Her attorney wants me there for the reading of the will on Friday. I'm surprised I was named in it."

"And where are you headed?" Garth asked his brother.

"A place called Black Crow, Wyoming."

"Do you need Regan to fly you there in the company plane? I can go along for support if you need it." Regan was the company pilot and Garth's wife. They had been married for nearly ten months.

"Black Crow is right outside of Laramie. I plan to gas up my plane and fly myself since it's less than a five-hour trip from here."

Cash and all his siblings had their pilot licenses. Due to Alaska's very limited road system, one of the most common ways of getting around was by aircraft. Locals liked to say that more Alaskans owned personal planes than cars.

"Okay, but if you change your mind, let me know."

"I will."

Two days later, Cash flew his Cessna to the Laramie Regional Airport. He'd ordered a rental car to be there when he arrived, and it was. Shifting his cell phone to the other ear, he tossed his overnight bag in the back seat as he continued his conversation with his sister, Charm. She was calling from Australia with her condolences.

Charm had tagged along with Garth's best friend, Walker Rafferty, and his wife, Bailey, on a trip to visit Bailey's sister, Gemma, who lived in Australia.

"Thanks, Charm, but you know the real deal with this. It's not like me and Ellen had a close relationship. Like I told Garth, I'm surprised she remembered I existed long enough to put me in a will."

Cash glanced at his watch before starting the car and switching the phone call to the vehicle's speaker system. He would get a good night's sleep, and be at the meeting with the attorney in the morning at eleven. Then he would leave, head back to the airport and fly home to Fairbanks.

"I need to end the call, Charm, so I can concentrate

on following the directions to Black Crow. I'll talk to you later, kid."

As Cash headed for the interstate, he thought about the conversation he'd had with his father before leaving. Bart was typical Bart. Even with six adult offspring, their old man still assumed it was his God-given right to stick his nose into their business when it didn't concern him.

Cash had put Bart in his place just that morning when he'd tried telling Cash to make sure he got everything his mother owned because it was rightly due him. Cash had made it clear to Bart that he didn't want a single thing. He'd even seriously thought about not showing up for the reading of the will. As far as he was concerned, it was too late for Ellen to make up for the years she had been absent from his life. The only reason he had decided to come was for closure.

The drive from Laramie to Black Crow took less than an hour. He couldn't help wondering when his mother had moved to Wyoming. According to Bart, when she left Fairbanks thirty-four years ago, she had moved to New York.

Cash saw the marker denoting the entrance into Black Crow's city limits, and recalled all he'd learned from doing an internet search last night before going to bed. It had first been inhabited by the Black Crow Indian tribe, from which the town derived its name. The present population was less than two thousand people, and most fought to retain an old-town feel, which was evident by the architecture of the buildings. He'd read that if any of the inhabitants thought Black Crow wasn't progressive enough for them, they were quickly invited to leave. But few people left and most had lived in the area for years. It was a close-knit place.

He came to a traffic light and watched numerous people walking around, going into the various shops. As he sat there, tapping his hand on the steering wheel, his gaze homed in on a woman who was walking out of an ice-cream shop. She was strikingly beautiful. He couldn't help noticing how she worked her mouth on her ice-cream cone, and he could just imagine her working her mouth on him the same way.

Cash drew in a deep breath as he shifted in the seat. She looked pretty damn good in her pullover sweater and a pair of jeans. If she was a sampling of what Black Crow had to offer, then maybe he needed to hang around for another day or two and not be so quick to leave town tomorrow.

He chuckled, thinking it would take more than a beautiful face and a gorgeous body to keep him in this town. Besides, he doubted that even if he stayed he'd be able to find her. He had more to do with his time than chase down a woman. Chances were, she was wearing some guy's ring. There was no way a woman who looked like her was not spoken for.

The driver behind him beeped his horn to let Cash know the traffic light had changed and it was time to move on. Not able to resist temptation, he glanced back for one final look at the woman and saw she was gone.

Just as well.

Brianna Banks entered the attorney's office the next morning. "Good morning, Lois."

The older woman glanced up at Brianna and smiled. "Good morning, Brianna. You're early."

"Is Mr. Cavanaugh in?"

"Yes, he's here, and since you and Mr. Outlaw are the only two needed for the reading of the will, we can get started as soon as he arrives." Lois Inglese then leaned over the desk and said in a low voice, "I didn't know Ellen had a son. Did you?"

Brianna drew in a deep breath. She liked Lois. Had known the fifty-something-year-old woman all her life. The one thing she also knew was that Lois had a penchant for gossip. More than once, Lois had gotten in hot water with Mr. Cavanaugh for discussing things that should be confidential.

"I'd rather not say, Lois." Brianna checked her watch. "If you don't mind, I'll take a seat over there and wait."

Lois's smile faded when she realized Brianna would not divulge any information.

Brianna crossed the room to take a chair by the window that overlooked Eagle Bend River. Although she had known about Ellen's son, Lois was the last person Brianna would admit anything to. She'd also known of their strained relationship, which was the main reason Brianna was prepared to not like him. Besides, there was a chance he might not show up today.

She picked up a magazine, deciding that whether the man showed up was not her concern. Brianna was thankful that Ellen had thought enough of her to include her in the will. She would appreciate whatever Ellen left for her.

Everything Brianna had done for Ellen in her final

days had been because Brianna had wanted to do so. Ellen had been there for her when she'd been a kid who lived on the Blazing Frontier Dude Ranch. Brianna's mother had managed the ranch and her father had been head foreman.

Brianna glanced up when the door opened and a tall, handsome man walked in. She recognized him immediately. She had seen a picture of him once, when he'd been ten years or so younger. She'd thought he was a hottie then. However, the man she saw now was so strikingly handsome, she could say she had never seen a man who looked that gorgeous before in her life.

The man was none other than Ms. Ellen's son, Cashen Outlaw.

From where Brianna was sitting, on the other side of the huge potted plant, he couldn't see her, which gave her the perfect opportunity to ogle him. He was dressed to the nines in a dark business suit. Very few men in Black Crow wore business suits; they probably didn't even own one. That included the attorneys and politicians. This was strictly a jeans and Western shirt town. Heck, they didn't even dress up for church.

The only time she saw a man in a suit these days was at funerals or when she drove into Laramie. Even Jackson, which was considered the top city in Wyoming when it came to education, jobs and other amenities, still had a very casual dress code. But she had no problem looking at this man, especially when the suit appeared tailor-made just for him.

She figured his height was every bit of six-two or three, and all she saw was his profile. That was enough to send sensations she hadn't felt in months—even years—flowing through her. She couldn't hear exactly what he was saying to Lois, but it was obvious the older woman was hanging on his every word. That proved a woman was never too old to appreciate a nice-looking man.

She really couldn't blame Lois. Cashen Outlaw had a commanding presence. A prime example of raw male power and self-confidence.

At that moment Henry Cavanaugh's office door opened and the older man, who'd been practicing law in Black Crow before Brianna was born, stepped out wearing jeans and a crisply starched chambray shirt.

Mr. Cavanaugh smiled at her and said, "Hello, Brianna." He shook her hand before moving toward the other man, introducing himself.

That is when Cashen glanced over at her, seeing her for the first time. The moment their gazes connected she felt weak in the knees. Lordy, he had beautiful almond-colored skin, a striking pair of dark eyes and hair that was neatly trimmed. He had a square-cut jaw and a wide, firm mouth with full lips that was perfect for his face. What really had her heart racing was a sexy pair of dimples that came into full display when he smiled.

He moved to stand beside Mr. Cavanaugh, and she saw how well his suit accentuated his solid frame. She had a feeling he would look absolutely male in anything he wore. And he smelled good. She was certain the arousing scent was him and not Mr. Cavanaugh.

"Let me introduce the two of you," Mr. Cavanaugh was saying, breaking into her thoughts. "Cashen Outlaw, this is Brianna Banks. She is the other person named in your mother's will."

If Mr. Cavanaugh's revelation surprised him, the man didn't show it. He merely extended his hand out to her. "Nice meeting you, Brianna."

"Same here, Cashen."

His smiled widened a fraction when he said, "Please, just Cash."

"Cash," she repeated, not able to tear her gaze from his. He was still holding her hand and his touch felt downright overwhelming.

"The two of you can step into my office."

With Mr. Cavanaugh's statement, Cash released her hand and said, "After you, Brianna."

"Thank you."

She followed Mr. Cavanaugh, and Cash brought up the rear. She did not have to glance over at Lois to know the older woman's eyes had watched their every move. At the moment Brianna didn't care. Her main concern was how she would share the same space with Cash Outlaw and keep herself from drooling.

Two

It's her.

Brianna Banks was the woman Cash had seen yesterday licking that ice-cream cone. The woman whose mouth he had fantasized about ever since. And she had known Ellen? In what capacity? Since she was here for the reading of the will, he hoped like hell she wasn't a sister he hadn't known about. He would soon find out.

They were sitting in front of Henry Cavanaugh's desk. The man had opened a folder and was flipping through papers. Brianna was staring straight ahead, and Cash was staring at her. At that moment he couldn't stop even if he wanted to.

And she isn't wearing a ring.

He thought the same thing now that he had thought when he'd seen her yesterday. She was simply gorgeous. Everything about her was a heart-stopper.

Whether it was the dark curly hair on her head that seemed to lie perfectly around her shoulders, or her striking features or her long, regal neck.

As if she sensed him staring, she glanced over at him and their gazes met. She had a gorgeous pair of dark eyes, a delicately shaped nose and glossy lips, beautifully shaped, succulent and sexy. They were perfect for her face. Perfect for her ice cream. Perfect for his—

"Okay, Cash and Brianna, I am ready to begin."

Mr. Cavanaugh's words had him snatching his gaze from hers.

"'I, Ellen Cashen Embelin, hereby bequeath all my possessions to the following. To my son, Cashen Outlaw, I am leaving you the Blazing Frontier Dude Ranch and the acres it sits on. This will include the barns, detached cottages and contents. Cashen, I am also leaving you all the animals, inventory, merchandise and vehicles. Furthermore, I am leaving you all the proceeds from my insurance policies with Mission Care Mutual and one half of whatever funds I have in my checking and savings accounts, my stocks, bonds and investment portfolio. The other half goes to Brianna Banks.'"

Mr. Cavanaugh paused a minute as he flipped over the sheet of paper. "'To Brianna Banks. In addition to those things named earlier, I am leaving you the foreman house that your parents lived in, that you are now living in, all its contents and the fifty acres it sits upon. I am also leaving you the additional fifty acres that connect to the Blazing Frontier Dude Ranch and back into the Keystone River. I am asking that both you and

Cashen, together, go through my personal things, including the boxes in the attic, and jointly decide how the items will be disposed of. This is not a stipulation but a request.'"

Mr. Cavanaugh released a deep sigh and then said, "That's the end of it and should cover everything. I am giving both of you copies of the will." He handed them packets. "Also included is a land surveyor diagram of the one hundred acres that were a part of the Blazing Frontier properties that you now own, Brianna. Are there any questions?"

Cash had one. He still did not know what relationship Brianna had with Ellen. While Cavanaugh had been reciting the will, Cash had seen the tears falling down her cheeks. Curiosity got the best of him.

"Yes, I have one," he said.

"And what is your question, Cash?" Mr. Cavanaugh asked, looking at him intently while leaning back in his chair.

"My question is for Brianna," he said, switching his gaze from Mr. Cavanaugh to her. "What was your relationship to my mother?"

Brianna was so touched by what Ellen had left her in the will that she was too overwhelmed to speak. It took her a moment to pull herself together before she could answer Cash.

"My parents worked at the Blazing Frontier Dude Ranch. My father worked as foreman even before it was a dude ranch, for over forty years, and my mother, close to thirty as ranch manager. As part of Dad's employment, they got to live in the foreman's house.

That's the house I was raised in, and the house Ms. Ellen just left for me in her will. Mom died five years ago while I was in college. After college I returned home and replaced her as ranch manager."

"What about your father? Is he still foreman?"

"No. My father died last year."

"I'm sorry to hear that."

"Thanks."

Brianna wondered if he'd asked her because he intended to contest the will. What Ellen had left her—half of her financial assets, the house and one hundred acres of land—had been way too generous.

Cash then turned his attention back to Mr. Cavanaugh. "I have no other questions, but it would help if you could recommend a good real estate agent in the area."

The older man lifted a brow. "Real estate agent?"

"Yes, I would like to put the ranch up for sale as soon as possible."

"But you haven't seen it," Brianna said, even though she didn't have a right to question him.

Cash evidently thought the same thing when he switched his gaze to her. The smile was no longer in his eyes. "I don't need to see it, Brianna. I have no desire to own a dude ranch. Is it still even operational?"

"Not at the moment," Brianna said, trying to hide her disappointment, but knowing she should not be surprised he didn't want the ranch. "It was closed down when Ellen's health began failing. But it can be operational again. When it was open, we operated at full capacity and always had a waiting list."

She was certain Cash heard the excitement in her

voice, but he merely nodded and said, "All of that is interesting, but I still plan to sell it."

"I hate to scurry you two off, but I have another appointment in a few minutes," Henry Cavanaugh said, breaking into their conversation, as he glanced at his watch. "You are welcome to use one of my conference rooms if you'd like to continue the conversation."

Brianna could see Cash's mind was made up. She was about to say there was no reason for them to continue their conversation when Cash spoke.

"Continuing the conversation is a great idea, but I prefer not to use one of your conference rooms." He then turned to Brianna Banks. "Would you join me for lunch?"

"Is there a place you suggest, Brianna?" Cash asked as they stepped out of Mr. Cavanaugh's office.

"There is a café if you like hamburgers. Monroe's. And they have the best fries."

He smiled. "I love hamburgers and fries."

"We won't have to move our cars since it's in walking distance. Right on the corner."

"Okay."

When they were leaving, Lois smiled at them before saying, "I hope the two of you have a good day."

"You as well, Lois," Brianna said when Cash opened the door for her. She had a feeling news about Cash would be all over town by evening.

"Is it always this windy here?" he asked, tightening his jacket as they walked.

Brianna tightened hers as well. "Yes, and the wind

today is rather mild. There is a scientific reason for all the wind."

He glanced over at her. "Is there?"

"Yes. The town is located right between the mountains. Instead of blocking the wind, the mountains make it move faster. Then the high air pressure across the Great Basin and lower pressure in the Plains make it stronger. This is mild. The worst of it is during the winter. Can you imagine all that wind combined with snow?"

He chuckled. "I can but I'd rather not. Alaska has its own weather issues."

"Yet you like living there?"

"I love it. It's home for me, and I'm used to the harsh weather. I can't imagine living anywhere else. Though I did live in Massachusetts while getting my master's degree from Harvard."

"In what field?" she asked him.

"Engineering." He looked over at her. "What college did you attend and what was your field of study?"

"I have a bachelor's degree in business administration from Clark Atlanta University," she said when they reached the corner. They paused for the traffic light to change before crossing the street.

"How did you like living in Atlanta?"

"It was quite an experience. I had never been anywhere other than Wyoming. I even thought of staying and getting a job there. But then Mom died in my senior year and it seemed to take me forever to fly back home for Dad. After her funeral, I returned to school just long enough to graduate. Then I returned to Black Crow and haven't left since."

They reached the café. "We're here."

He positioned his body next to her to block the wind and opened the door. She would admit the warmth from the huge fireplace felt inviting today. "We can grab that table over there, Cash," she said and led him toward it.

Brianna didn't miss the interest they were generating as they crossed the room. Most of the people knew her, but they didn't know him. Not yet anyway. Lois would make sure they did before nightfall.

"Nice view," he said, glancing out the window. "This town sure has a lot of lakes."

She smiled. "Yes, we do. There are six in all, not counting the ones on the outskirts of town where most of the ranching is. Then there is the Keystone River. Most people who come here for the first time say Black Crow is definitely one of Wyoming's best-kept secrets."

After their waitress brought their drinks and took their order, Brianna glanced up from sipping her tea to find Cash staring at her. The dark eyes holding hers were mysterious and breathtaking—hypnotic. She broke eye contact with him to get her bearings.

"So," he said, returning to their previous conversation, "you've never felt adventurous? Wanted to go other places? Visit other states? See the world?"

She shrugged.

There was no need to tell him there had been a time when she thought she would get that opportunity. That's when she and Alan Dawkins had been together. They had dated all through high school and he had graduated the year before her. Their goal had been for him to join the army after high school and then return to Black Crow when she graduated the following year. They would marry and she would be an army wife, the mother of his children, and travel the world with him.

Things didn't quite work out that way. While stationed in Germany, Alan met someone. He had returned home the year she had graduated like he had promised, but he'd brought his German wife with him. At least he'd had the decency to write to tell her beforehand. Everyone in town had pitied her and had considered Alan's betrayal unforgiveable. That's why her parents had encouraged her to put as much distance between her and Black Crow as she could for college. They figured Atlanta, Georgia, would be far enough.

"Maybe at one time I did," she finally answered, "but I got over it."

It was then that the waitress delivered their lunch.

Three

Cash enjoyed the delicious hamburger and fries, but found he was enjoying Brianna's company even more. He loved the sound of her voice and definitely liked looking at her. And if he thought her mouth was incredible, then her eyes followed closely. Whenever she looked at him, they exuded a sensuality that she probably didn't even know she had. If she did, she wouldn't look at him the way he'd caught her doing.

It had gotten quiet between them but now that their meal was almost over, he got down to the real reason he had invited her to lunch. He wanted to know more about her.

But before he could ask her a question, she said, "I guess you want me to tell you all about Ms. Ellen."

He took a sip of his water. He could certainly see how she assumed that, but she was wrong. There was nothing he wanted to know about the woman who had deserted him thirty-four years ago. He'd rather she told him more about herself, but he had time, so he would let her tell him about Ellen first.

"What do you want to tell me? It's been thirty-four years since I last saw her."

"Not since you were a baby, right?"

He lifted a brow, wondering how much she knew. "You've known Ellen for your whole life, for twenty-three years, right?"

"Close to twenty-eight. I have a birthday coming up this summer."

She was twenty-seven? She definitely looked a lot younger. Her copper-colored skin was smooth, soft, ageless and flawless.

"How long were she and Van Embelin married?"

"Ten years before he died. Mr. Van was older than Ms. Ellen by seventeen years, but they were very dedicated to each other. My parents said she made him feel young again. Restored his vitality. Made him smile."

Cash lifted a brow. "He had stopped smiling?"

"Yes. When his wife died of cancer, he became a recluse for close to five years. Ms. Ellen brought him out of it."

Cash paused and then asked, "Did Ellen tell you how long it'd been since she'd seen me?" He convinced himself that he was only asking out of curiosity.

"I understand she took your father to court for custody of you and lost."

"Yes, that's true." Cash decided not to go into how Bart managed to do that during a time when most courts sympathized with the mother. Cash and his brothers were well aware that in Bart's world, their father had had the money and the means to do whatever the hell he wanted to do and usually did. However, that did not excuse Ellen not reaching out to him at some point over the past thirty-four years. She had known where he was. Someone definitely knew how to contact Bart when she passed away.

"Was the Blazing Frontier always a dude ranch?" he asked, to take the subject off him.

Brianna's smile brightened. "No. Turning it into a dude ranch was Ellen's idea. At first the town balked at the idea, knowing that meant a lot of tourists in town, and they weren't sure they would like it. But Ellen somehow convinced them it would be good for the economy and to give it a try for a year. After that time, if the dude ranch had a negative effect on the town, then they would go back to regular ranching."

Cash took a sip of his lemonade. "I take it things went well."

"Better than anyone expected. Even the naysayers had to concede having the dude ranch on the outskirts of town was a great idea. It attracted people who appreciated the Old West and wanted to recapture those times. Those tourists often came into town and spent money. Lots of it." She paused. "The economy took a hit when the ranch shut down. The people of Black Crow would love for it to reopen."

Cash knew what Brianna was hinting at. Evidently, he hadn't made himself clear in Henry Cavanaugh's office. Hopefully he would this time. "Then I'm hoping whoever buys it will make it back into a dude ranch. Let's just hope there is an interested buyer."

Brianna frowned. "Oh, trust me, there will definitely be an interested buyer."

Under other circumstances he would be glad to hear that, but from her tone he had a feeling the person Brianna suspected would want to buy it was someone she'd rather not own it. Cash didn't say anything, refusing to get involved in small-town drama. It didn't matter to him who bought the ranch as long as the sale was quick.

When the waitress returned to remove their plates, he said, "Mr. Cavanaugh never did mention the name of a real estate agent. Possibly you can."

Her frown deepened. "Are you really going to sell the Blazing Frontier without even taking the time to look at it? It's a beautiful place."

"I'm sure it is, but I have no need of a ranch, dude or otherwise."

"I think you're making a mistake, Cash."

Cash lifted a brow. Normally, he didn't care what any person, man or woman, thought about any decision he made, but for some reason what she thought mattered.

It shouldn't.

What he should do was thank her for joining him for lunch, and tell her not to walk back to Cavanaugh's office with him, although he knew both their cars were parked there. In other words, he should put as much distance between them as possible.

I can't.

Maybe it was the way her luscious mouth tightened when she was not happy about something. He'd picked up on it twice now. Lord help him but he didn't want to see it a third time. He'd rather see her smile, lick an ice-cream cone or…lick him.

He quickly forced the last image from his mind but not before a hum of lust shot through his veins. There had to be a reason he was so attracted to her. Maybe he could blame it on the Biggins deal Garth had closed just months before he'd gotten engaged to Regan. That had taken working endless days and nights, and for the past year Cash's social life had been practically nonexistent.

On the other hand, even without the Biggins deal as an excuse, there was strong sexual chemistry radiating between them. He felt it, but honestly wasn't sure that even at twenty-seven she recognized it for what it was.

That was intriguing, to the point that he was tempted to hang around Black Crow another day. Besides, he was a businessman, and no businessman would sell or buy anything without checking it out first. He was letting his personal emotions around Brianna cloud what was usually a very sound business mind.

"You are right, Brianna. I would be making a mistake if I didn't at least see the ranch before selling it. Is now a good time?"

The huge smile that spread across her face was priceless…and mesmerizing. When was the last time a woman, any woman, had this kind of effect on him? When he felt spellbound? He concluded that never had a woman captivated him like Brianna Banks was doing.

"Not sure if today would be okay with you dressed as you are now. Unless you brought a pair of jeans with you."

He chuckled, knowing she had a point. "I didn't,

but I'm sure there's a store in town where I can purchase more clothes."

"Of course. Roy's Circle O is only two doors down and has a good selection of items."

Cash nodded. When he returned to Alaska, he would have no reason to ever return here. No reason to ever see her again. So, the way he saw it, he could definitely wait another couple days to leave. "How about if we get together tomorrow morning around ten? Will you be available to show me around the ranch then?"

If he had thought her smile could not get any more enchanting, he'd been wrong. With that kind of smile, he would give her practically anything just to see it on those sensuous lips.

"Yes, I'll be available, and it's best to see it by horseback. Can you ride a horse?"

He could not help but return her smile. "Yes, I can ride and I look forward to seeing you again in the morning, Brianna."

Brianna was in a good mood when she got home an hour or so later. Ms. Ellen had certainly made her day with what she had left Brianna in the will. Now she was looking forward to showing Cash Outlaw around the Blazing Frontier tomorrow. She hoped that once he saw the ranch for himself he would want to keep it.

There was no doubt in her mind that once Hal Sutherland heard the ranch was for sale, he would jump at the chance to buy it. Hal was Mr. Van Embelin's nephew—his first wife's brother's son. Hal had never wanted Mr. Van to remarry, hoping that would make him Mr. Van's heir. Then the Blazing Frontier would one day be his. Hal's property bordered the Blazing Frontier.

Needless to say, Hal hadn't been happy when Mr. Van had married Ms. Ellen. When Mr. Van died, Hal offered to buy the ranch. He didn't think Ms. Ellen had the grit to operate a working ranch. Ms. Ellen, with Brianna's parents' help, along with all the ranch hands who'd become loyal to her, proved Hal wrong. He hadn't liked that either and tried causing problems.

When Ms. Ellen became ill, Hal again figured he would be her heir. After all, it had been his family's land originally. Hal had begun boasting about what he planned to do with the Blazing Frontier even before Ellen had taken her last breath.

Brianna figured he would know by now—thanks to Lois—that the reading of Ms. Ellen's will had occurred today and since he hadn't been summoned to the reading, he was not in the will. Hal probably also would discover, at the same time most of the townspeople did, that Ellen had left mostly everything, including the Blazing Frontier, to her son. A son only very few people knew about.

Now it seemed Hal might get the land anyway, although he would have to pay for it. He wouldn't like the fact that Ms. Ellen had left those fifty acres on the Keystone River to Brianna. Ellen had to have known those fifty acres and the waterway were vital if anyone ever turned the dude ranch back into a working ranch for cattle. Without water access, the cows would die of thirst unless the owners came up with another alternative to provide adequate water to their herds.

If Cash sold the ranch to Hal, she anticipated noth-

ing but endless drama for her. Hal was a mean ras-
cal who was used to getting what he wanted—except
from his fearless adversary, Ms. Ellen, who refused to
let him bully her.

After leaving the café, she and Cash had walked
back to their cars. Instead of leaving right away as he'd
done, she had sat in her car and reread the papers Mr.
Cavanaugh had given to her. Everything was legal and
final. This house that her parents had never owned was
now hers.

Brianna had known about Cash because Ms. Ellen
had confided in her years ago. Brianna had begged
Ellen to let her contact Cash when her illness got
worse, but Ellen had refused. Before she died, Ellen
had given Brianna power of attorney to handle her
affairs until the reading of the will, and Brianna had
honored Ellen's wishes and hadn't contacted Cash.

Going into the kitchen, she poured a cup of coffee,
then grabbed the mail. She frowned when she saw one
letter that didn't have a return address.

Brianna was about to toss it aside when something
about the writing of her name gave her pause, made
her heartbeat kick up a notch. She quickly tore open
the letter. There was not a date to indicate when it had
been written. Her gaze focused on the words scrawled
in bold handwriting…

Remember your promise,
Dad

Brianna's breath caught and she fought back tears.
Without a shadow of a doubt she knew her father had

indeed written to her. But who had he entrusted to send her the reminder? Brian Banks had always been a likable person. Over the years while foreman her father had met a lot of people who'd made coming to the ranch every year a ritual. He could have reached out to one of them to send the letter to her.

It didn't really matter who her father had entrusted to send her the reminder. The message was clear.

Going into her living room, she slid down on the sofa, leaned back and closed her eyes to stop the tears. Sadness was overshadowing what had been a happy day for her.

It was here in this very room, while sitting on this same sofa beside her father and holding his frail hand, when she'd made him that promise. The night before he had passed away while watching his favorite Westerns on television. He had refused the chemo the doctors had advised him to get. Instead, he had chosen quality of life over quantity of life.

Although she had wished things were different, she had accepted his decision and had gone out of her way to make his last days as special and meaningful as possible.

Knowing his life was about to end, Brian Banks had been worried about his only child. He was concerned about what her life would be without him. More than anything he had wanted her to be happy. He asked her to promise him that by her thirtieth birthday she would not be alone.

Her father had known, more than anyone, about her dreams of forever with Alan, and he had known the one thing his daughter wanted more than anything was to one day become a mother.

While sitting on this sofa that night—his last one on earth—he had made her promise him that she would have the baby she wanted, with or without a husband, by her thirtieth birthday. Given how she felt about trusting her heart to another man, he'd known if she did have a child, it would be without the benefit of a husband. He had been fine with that and had given her his blessing. He had let her know that whatever it took to make her happy, he would support her, even in death.

Brianna wiped away her tears. Thanks to Ms. Ellen she now had a home to call her own and was in a better financial position to fulfill her promise and make her dream come true.

She would contact the fertility center's sperm bank to begin whatever paperwork was needed. She was going to have her baby.

Four

"Did you say a dude ranch?"

Cash switched his cell phone to the other ear while pulling the rawhide belt through the loops of the jeans he'd purchased yesterday. He had walked out of the store with a couple pairs of jeans and several Western shirts because Roy Dawkins, the owner of the shop, was a born salesman.

"Yeah, Garth, a dude ranch. I decided to stay a couple days longer to check out it before selling it."

"I would hope so. I can't believe you would even think of doing it any other way."

"I know, but…"

"But you want to unload anything Ellen left you. Keeping it will make it seem as if her not staying in touch was okay when you feel it wasn't."

Cash drew in a deep breath. There were times when

he thought Garth knew him better than he knew himself. "Yes, that's it. How did you know?"

"I've been there. Remember how my mother rejected me a few years ago when I decided to go see her? At least Ellen thought enough of you to leave you something. Jess's mother didn't leave him a single thing when she passed away four years ago, other than an elaborate New Orleans funeral to pay for. And I definitely can't see Sloan's or Maverick's mothers being generous either."

"I know, but a part of me wants to just leave here, Garth. The sooner the better. Even at the store yesterday, all I heard was what a kindhearted woman Ellen was. It took everything I had to let them know that as far as I was concerned, she was far from kindhearted."

"Well, the Ellen I remember was kind as well, Cash. Of all Bart's wives, I thought Ellen was the most decent. Definitely way too decent for Bart. She was always kind to me and Jess. Treated us like her own. I can't say the same about Sloan's and Maverick's mothers."

Not wanting to talk about the woman who'd given birth to him, Cash checked his watch. "Look, Garth, I'm supposed to meet someone at the ranch to take a tour of the place. I just wanted to let you know that I won't be returning home until tomorrow."

"Okay, Cash. Take care."

"I will."

After ending the call, Cash walked over to the window. It seemed like today would be a pretty nice Saturday, mostly because he would be seeing Brianna

Banks again. He had thought of her a lot since they had parted ways. More than he should have.

Like he'd told Garth, he would check out the land and then return home tomorrow. The last thing he would do was let anyone, especially a woman with a pretty face, weaken his resolve.

No matter what, the Blazing Frontier Dude Ranch would be sold.

Brianna was sitting in the porch swing when she saw the rental car coming up the long driveway. If Cash hadn't been impressed by the mile-long scenic drive he'd taken at the turnoff to Blazing Frontier, then he definitely would be once he saw the ranch house with the Rocky Mountains as a backdrop.

The huge three-story structure had been built years ago and renovated twice. The last time had been by Ms. Ellen. The purpose had been to house the guests who preferred staying at the main house instead of in one of the sixty cabins scattered around the property.

Due to Mr. Van's lingering leg injury from being thrown from a horse in his younger days, they'd resided on the first floor in their own wing. The other wing was where the check-in desk, dining room, kitchen and storage rooms were located.

Brianna stood when the car came to a stop. She had thought about Cash Outlaw a lot last night, convincing herself she'd only done so for worry of what he would think of the Blazing Frontier and if perhaps he would change his mind about selling it.

"Welcome to the Blazing Frontier," she said, smiling when he got out of the car.

It took everything she had not to weaken in the knees. She'd thought Cash looked good yesterday in a business suit, but the Cash dressed in jeans, a Western shirt, cowboy boots and a Stetson was almost too much for her cardiovascular system. She was certain more blood than needed was rushing through her veins. That had to be the reason she suddenly felt light-headed.

He had been transformed from an Alaskan businessman to a Wyoming cowboy. It was quite obvious his outfit had cost a pretty penny. When he made it up to the top step, her gazed roamed over him from head to toe. "It appears that Roy laid his salesmanship on thick."

Tilting his hat back, Cash grinned down at her. "Yes, you can definitely say that."

Brianna tucked her hands into the pockets of her jeans. She couldn't wait to hear his first impression. "So, what do you think so far?"

"I'll admit I was taken aback. I hadn't expected it to be so large."

She nodded, thinking he hadn't seen anything yet. She couldn't wait until they covered the area on horseback. "Let me show you the house."

The tour inside lasted well over an hour. For someone who hadn't been interested in even seeing the ranch, he was checking out every single detail. That could be a bad thing if he was noticing the needed repairs. She hoped his intense scrutiny was a good thing and that he thought the ranch was a smart investment regardless of any needed repairs.

While giving him a tour, she had shared the history of the ranch, including details of the last major renovations that had been done, and answered his questions. He had commented on the beautiful mountain view that was practically out of every window. She took that as a good sign.

They even went out back to the game center with pool tables, a place to play cards, a theater room and a library. "A number of people bring their kids here to introduce them to the Wild West at an early age," Brianna said. "A fun way to learn history. Usually those kids grow up and return with their kids. Most of the people who come here are regulars. For the past three years we weren't accepting any newcomers unless they were recommended by our regular guests."

The building next to the game center featured an old-fashioned saloon. On the opposite side of the house was a screen-enclosed swimming pool.

Cash admitted he had not expected to see that. "Another amenity for the kids?"

She smiled. "You would be surprised how many adults love to go swimming as a way to relax after riding the range."

When they made it back to the front porch, she said, "We can walk over to the barn and have one of the guys saddle up horses for us."

"There are still men working here?" he asked as he walked beside her.

"Only five. Ted Dennis is the man who took my dad's place as foreman and has worked here for fifteen years. He agreed to stay on until the ranch's fate was decided."

"And the other four men?"

"They are guys who have also worked here for

years. They are hoping you or the new owner will hire them on."

"I'd think it would be to the owner's advantage to do that. They would be getting experienced men who know the land."

Brianna didn't say anything. Evidently, he hadn't been impressed enough to keep it if he was still thinking of selling.

All five men were in the barn working and she introduced Cash to all of them. In no time at all, Ted had the horses saddled and ready for them to use.

They started out at a trot and Brianna had to inwardly admit she was impressed with Cash's horsemanship. She had to believe that once they got out on the range, if nothing else had impressed him so far, it would.

He was impressed.

Cash honestly didn't know what to say as he rode beside Brianna, so he didn't say anything at all. Instead, he took it all in. He hadn't known. Hadn't had a clue about the size of the spread Ellen had left him. It wasn't just the size—it was the sheer beauty of the surroundings.

He recalled the first time he had visited Westmoreland Country with his brothers. Westmoreland Country was the section on the outskirts of Denver where his cousins the Westmorelands lived, and it encompassed eighteen hundred acres. This property here was larger than that. Nearly double.

And it was the most beautiful land he had ever seen. Numerous streams, several apple orchards, several caverns, rich valleys, glassy plains and an abundance of mountains. Then there was the Keystone River, at least a small section of it. He could see why the Blazing Frontier Dude Ranch had been so popular. It was a Westerner's paradise.

They had dismounted to walk to the lake. He tossed a pebble across the waters and watched it skip across the surface. He glanced over at Brianna. She was an accomplished rider. He'd watched how she'd jumped the small streams with the ease. "Where does this river lead to?" Cash asked her.

She had put on her own hat before they had headed out on horseback, and several strands of hair peeked out haphazardly around her face. He wondered if she knew just how beautiful she was. Even with a hat, she looked jaw-droppingly sexy. There was nothing serene or quiet about her looks.

He thought now what he'd thought that day he had seen her coming out of the ice-cream shop. There was no way a woman with her looks wasn't attached, regardless of the fact she wasn't wearing a ring.

The one thing he did know was that she'd once been Roy's cousin's girlfriend. He'd gotten that much from the man while shopping. Roy had said the two were supposed to get married right out of high school, but things hadn't worked out. Cash wondered why.

The reason wasn't really any of his business.

"This waterway leads to the bigger part of the Keystone River."

"Is that part of the Blazing Frontier property as well?" he asked.

She glanced over at him. "It used to be. That's the

section of land Ellen bequeathed to me." She turned and pointed east. "Although you can't see it, my house is over there, behind those huge oak trees."

He nodded. Ellen had definitely been generous to her, and after what she'd told him yesterday, he was glad. Her parents had worked for years for the Blazing Frontier. It seemed fitting that she reap some of the benefits.

Brianna explained there was another section to show him. They rode awhile. Then suddenly he brought his horse to a stop and she did the same. The view, for as far as his eyes could see, was magnificent. Spellbinding. Simply breathtaking.

He didn't say anything for a long moment. He just sat there and took it all in. Moments passed before she finally spoke.

"So, Cash. What do you think?"

He looked at her. First of all, he thought Brianna was the most desirable woman he'd ever met. Of course, she wasn't asking what he thought of *her*, but he couldn't let that private thought slip by. Cash knew what she was really asking, but still, he would not tell her anything definite. "I admit I'm impressed, Brianna. I honestly did not expect to see all of this. It's beautiful."

He paused. "Do you know Hal Sutherland?" The tensing of her shoulders and the way her lips tightened were telling. Obviously, Hal Sutherland was someone she didn't too much care for. An old boyfriend, perhaps?

"Yes, I know him. Why?"

"He called me at the hotel last night, ready to make an offer. Told me to name my price."

"I'm sure he did. He's been trying to get his hands on the Blazing Frontier for years."

Cash nodded. "I see."

"Now I have a question for you, Cash."

"Which is?"

"What about Ms. Ellen's request that the two of us go through her personal belongings and decide what to do with them?"

"I honestly don't want to be involved in that. Whatever you decide to do with Ellen's things is fine with me." Then, barely missing a beat, he said, "It's time to head back."

"I am so happy Ms. Ellen looked out for you in her will, Brie. What she did was so thoughtful and kind. Did you have any idea she was going to do that?"

Brianna took a sip of her lemonade while talking to her best friend, Miesha James. It was a beautiful Sunday afternoon after the downpour late yesterday evening.

"Yes, that was kind and thoughtful of her, and no, I had no idea she would do that."

"Tell me about Cashen Outlaw, now that you've seen him in the flesh. Was he worth the crush you had on him years ago?"

Brianna rolled her eyes. Only Miesha would remember that. Brianna had finished her first year of college, hurt and humiliated after Alan's betrayal. In the summer she had returned home and she'd rarely left the ranch, wanting to retreat from a world filled with pain and self-pity. One day after volunteering to organize Ms. Ellen's attic, she'd come across a private investigator's report that had included a photograph of Cash. It was his graduation picture from college. She had gotten hooked by his huge smile, and on that day he had become her fantasy boyfriend. Daydreaming about Cash all that summer had helped her get over the pain Alan had caused.

Brianna smiled. "Yes. I can sum up Cashen Outlaw in one word. *Hot*."

"Now you got my bones shivering in lust, girl. Was he really that hot?"

"Yes. Everything about him. His features, his body, his clothes, the way he carried himself. Even the way he rode his horse. However, that picture I saw of him when he was in his early twenties is nothing like the thirtysomething hunk he's aged into. Like I said, he is hot."

"Um…maybe I need to come pay you a visit."

Brianna chuckled. "Too late. He left this morning to return to Alaska and there is no reason for him to come back. In fact, I got the distinct impression that he won't ever return."

"Didn't you say Ms. Ellen left him the ranch?"

"Yes, but he doesn't want it. He'd made up his mind to sell it before even seeing it. After giving him a tour yesterday, I could tell he was impressed, but I doubt he was impressed enough to keep it." She paused, then added, "He did say Hal Sutherland had already contacted him and made an offer."

"Hal Sutherland! Did you tell him what a douche-bag that man is?"

"No, and I don't intend to. I will not influence Cash in any way…not that I think I could. Cash is a business-man. For him it will be all about business."

"I think you should tell him."

"I disagree. Can we change the subject?"

"One more question. Did Cashen Outlaw say why he never reached out to his mom over the years? Why he never answered her letters?"

"No, and I didn't ask him. I did just what I promised Ms. Ellen I would do if our paths ever crossed and that was to not bring it up to him and not pass judgment on him because of it. The latter was hard."

"I'm sure it was."

"I want to believe, like Ms. Ellen did, that the letters never reached him. That his father made sure of it."

"That's why you should mention the letters to him, Brie."

"I promised Ms. Ellen I wouldn't."

"You and your promises."

"I know. I know. And speaking of promises, I have some news to share with you," Brianna said, refilling her glass with lemonade.

"What?"

"Now that I know I have a roof over my head for keeps, I'm moving ahead with plans to have a baby. Dad sent me a reminder of that promise on Friday."

"Your dad?"

"Yes." Brianna told Miesha about the letter.

"Wow, Brie. You don't know who sent it?"

"No, and really that doesn't matter because it could be anyone. Dad had a lot of friends who would do whatever he asked. It's good knowing he supports my decision. Now what I want to know is—since you had the procedure six years ago, are there any regrets?"

There was a pause before Miesha said, "Darrett is my world and I won't ever regret giving birth to him. But…"

"But what?"

"If I had to do it over again, I would go about it differently."

Brianna lifted a brow. "In what way?"

"I wouldn't use a sperm bank."

Brianna frowned. She recalled Miesha telling her how easy using a sperm bank had been. She'd filled out the questionnaire indicating the specific traits she wanted her child to have, even down to the eye color. Then they'd selected a donor based on her preference. "Why?"

"Because Darrett is getting older, and now that he's in the first grade and other kids have fathers, he wants to know about his. I wish I had a picture of a real person I could show him instead of a photo of a test tube." Brianna heard the sorrow in her friend's voice when she added, "If I had it to do all over again, Brianna, I would use a human being and go through the process of procreation the traditional way."

"Yes, but that way can get messy," Brianna said. "Very few men would voluntarily get a woman pregnant, Miesha. They would envision eighteen years of child support."

"Yes, but I'd take my time and find a guy who would go along with my plan. There are guys out there who want to be fathers without the benefit of a wife, just like there are women who want to be mothers without the benefit of a husband. The key is to find the right man."

Miesha paused and then said, "And if you find a man who's willing to meet you halfway, one who will sign papers agreeing that you won't ever hit him up for child support or the like, then I'd consider going that route as well." She chuckled and tacked on, "And if the sex is good, then that will be a bonus."

Later that night, as Brianna got ready for bed, she thought about what Miesha had told her. Her friend had definitely given her food for thought, although Brianna had completed the paperwork with the fertility clinic online last night. She had decided on the one in Jackson. The one in Laramie was too close for comfort since a lot of people living in Black Crow commuted to Laramie for work. The last thing she needed was anyone getting into her business.

Brianna drew in a deep breath. She didn't have long to make whatever decisions she was going to make. She would be twenty-eight in a few months and there was no guarantee she would get pregnant right away. Waiting too long would be pushing things too close to her thirtieth birthday for comfort.

When Brianna settled in bed, she knew there was not anyone living in these parts that she would want to father her child. Most of the guys she'd dated over the past couple years she considered nothing more than friends. And she didn't want to fall in love. One heartbreak was enough.

As she drifted off to sleep, the vision of a particular man floated through her mind. Cash Outlaw. She hoped he'd made it back home safely.

Five

"You really inherited a dude ranch, Cash, and are honestly thinking about selling it?"

Cash glanced over at his brother Maverick, but noticed Sloan and Garth seemed as interested in what his youngest brother had asked. They had just finished their weekly Monday midday meeting at Outlaw Freight Lines in one of the conference rooms.

Usually, as soon as the meeting ended, they would quickly scatter to their own respective offices to continue to tackle whatever had been on their agenda for that day. However, it seemed his brothers were more interested in hearing what he had to say than doing their own work. Even Garth, who knew a little more about the situation than the others.

Cash had spoken with Garth before he toured the

ranch on Saturday, so Cash figured Garth was only wondering if his decision had changed since then.

"Blazing Frontier is definitely a nice spread, and it's even more enormous than I'd assumed. I admit that I've never seen so much beautiful land anywhere."

Sloan lifted a brow. "Even compared to Westmoreland Country?"

"Yes, but in a different way. The Blazing Frontier is twice the size, so there is more open land, with the Rockies in the background. It's wilderness and frontier."

"You inherited that much property?" Sloan asked in amazement.

"Yes. However, Ellen did bequeath a house and the one hundred acres it sits on to a woman by the name of Brianna Banks. Her parents worked on the Blazing Frontier for years. Brianna even worked there after college while it was a dude ranch. Ellen had a close relationship with Brianna and her parents."

"Are her parents still alive?" Sloan asked.

"No. They passed away."

"How old is this Brianna Banks?"

Cash glanced over at Maverick. He wasn't surprised this particular brother had asked. Maverick was a known womanizer. "She's twenty-seven."

"Is she pretty?" Maverick also wanted to know.

Cash held his brother's gaze. "Why?"

Maverick shrugged. "Just asking out of curiosity."

Cash didn't say anything for a minute. "Yes, Brianna Banks is pretty. In fact, she is *very* pretty."

"Did you hit on her?"

Cash rolled his eyes. "Not everybody is like you, Maverick."

A grin spread across Maverick's face. "And that's a good thing. Less competition means more women for me to enjoy.

"So, tell me more about this woman," Maverick said.

Cash glared at his brother. "Don't even think it, Maverick."

"Do I detect a little possessiveness in your tone?" Maverick asked, trying to get a rise out of Cash.

"No."

"Sounds like it."

Garth, who was known to bring peace whenever there was friction between the brothers, spoke up. "Have you decided if you're going to keep the property, Cash?"

Before Cash could answer, Sloan said, "Of course he's going to keep it."

Cash glanced over at his brother. "I am?"

Sloan countered with, "Why wouldn't you?"

Cash shrugged. "Although I can tell it was a nice dude ranch at one time, it's been shut down a little over a year. I noticed a number of repairs that need to be made to bring it back up to par. Not sure I want to put any money into doing all that needs to be done."

Maverick nodded. "Even if you decide not to re-open the dude ranch, just think of other things you can do with it. The Westmoreland cousins are always looking for more land for their horses. You can turn it into a horse ranch."

Cash knew this was true and had even given it some

thought on his flight back home on Sunday. Several of his Westmoreland cousins had partnered to operate a horse training and breeding company, and it was doing great financially. A number of the horses they'd trained had won several derbies over the years.

"I agree with Maverick. If I were you, I'd talk to the cousins," Sloan suggested. "And why limit yourself? With that much land it can be a dude ranch again, too. Heck, I'd even consider coming on as an investor."

Cash was surprised. "You would?"

"In a heartbeat."

"So would I," Maverick said, leaning back in his chair. "I spent time with a woman at a dude ranch in Texas a few years ago and really enjoyed the experience. Both in and out of the bedroom. You wouldn't believe how many Wild West enthusiasts there are. I think it would be a good investment."

"You could count me in as well," Garth said. "I'm sure something like that would interest Jess, too."

Cash was silent as he stared at his brothers. Some people found it amazing that the six Outlaw siblings were as close as they were, considering each one of them had a different mother. But that's the way it had always been, even when, collectively, they'd had to take on Bart. It had taken the six of them to convince Bart to retire as CEO of Outlaw Freight Lines after the board had threatened to oust him.

"You guys are serious, aren't you?" Cash asked his brothers.

"Yes," Garth said, nodding. "Granted, we haven't seen the place. We're going by what you're telling us. You might be sitting on a gold mine and not know it,

Cash. I agree with Sloan. If you want to turn it into a horse ranch, you'll have the Westmoreland cousins who will probably be interested. And if you decide to turn it back into a dude ranch, you'll have your brothers as investors."

"I want to see this place, Cash," Sloan said, rubbing his hands together excitedly.

"I think we all should," Garth added. "What about this weekend, Cash? I can call Jess to join us if he doesn't have any plans."

"This weekend will be great," Cash said. "We can all stay at the ranch house," he suggested, thrilled at the idea of going back to the ranch when he thought of a certain woman he would love seeing again…

"There's plenty of room. I'll call Brianna and have her hire someone to come in to make sure the place is ready for us. And I'll call the Westmoreland cousins to see if they'd like to join us. Then they can give me their expert opinions," Cash added.

Moments later they all left the conference room to head back to their respective offices. Cash was glad he had gotten Brianna's telephone number from her before they parted ways on Saturday. He would go so far as admitting that he had been thinking about her more than he wanted to, and had tried blocking any thoughts of her from his mind since returning to Alaska. So far nothing had worked.

Sitting down at his desk, he knew there had to be a reason for his acute attraction to her. An attraction that had him looking forward to this weekend. An attraction that had his fingers itching just to dial the phone so he could hear her voice.

When it came to women, he'd never considered anything remotely close to a serious relationship. It hadn't surprised Cash when Garth had settled down and married. Being the oldest, Garth had wanted to marry. As far as Cash was concerned, his oldest brother had hit the jackpot when he'd realized he loved Regan and took the initiative to do something about it. Now Garth was a happy man.

Their father had not set a good example when it came to love, marriage and happiness. Cash was glad Garth had not let that influence him. However, that didn't mean what worked for Garth would work for Cash, Jess, Sloan, Maverick or even Charm. They would have to find their own way when it came to settling down and having a future with someone or remaining single.

No matter how intense his attraction to Brianna, Cash didn't have the time or inclination to get involved in a serious relationship. But then, how serious could it get when she lived in Wyoming and he lived in Alaska?

Satisfied this attraction to Brianna Banks would eventually fizzle out, he reached for the phone to give her a call.

Brianna ended the call with Cash. She had been surprised to hear from him and even more surprised to hear that he would be returning to Black Crow this weekend with his brothers and cousins. He said there would be as many as fifteen of them in all. Did that mean he might be thinking about keeping the place?

He didn't say and she hadn't asked. The only thing

he'd done was request that she hire someone to prepare the ranch house for their visit. He'd also asked that Ted have additional horses available. She would call Hattie, who'd been over housekeeping at the ranch for years.

Cash had said he would be arriving early Friday and the others would arrive sometime Friday evening. Everyone would be staying until Sunday. That meant it would be an all-weekend affair. Fifteen men could consume a lot of food. She would call Dano, who'd been the ranch's chef, to make sure the refrigerators were stocked. Should she suggest that Dano be available to cook meals, too?

No, she had to slow down. Otherwise, she would be calling the entire Blazing Frontier staff. It wouldn't be fair to give them false hope when she had no idea of Cash's intentions. He might merely have planned a weekend with his brothers and cousins as a guys' getaway before he officially sold it.

However, what if he was still deciding? The more impressed he was, the better, and when it came to good cooking, Dano definitely knew how to impress.

A few hours later, all the calls had been made. Long ago, with her parents' help, Brianna had understood the meaning of teamwork when it came to the Blazing Frontier. She'd also come to understand the meaning of dedication and loyalty. That's why everyone she'd called had been eager to come back and do what they could to make Cash Outlaw's weekend at the ranch one he wouldn't forget.

Standing, she grabbed the pail to pick some fresh

apples when her phone rang. The number wasn't one she recognized, but she answered anyway.

"Hello?"

"May I speak with Brianna Banks, please?" the feminine voice said on the other end.

"This is Brianna. Banks."

"Ms. Banks, this is Sally Harper at the fertility clinic in Jackson. We got your paperwork and are in the process of reviewing it now."

Brianna smiled. "Yes, Ms. Harper. Is there anything else I need to do?"

"No. We will start looking through our database to see if there's a donor who fits the profile you've requested."

She told Ms. Harper she wanted to move quickly, and the woman suggested they set up an appointment for Brianna's physical for next Thursday. Less than ten minutes later, she ended her call with Sally Harper, telling herself that although she'd taken into account everything Miesha had said, she wasn't sure she wanted to know the identity of her baby's father.

Picking up the pail on the table, she headed outside. Today had certainly been a day for good news. Her application for a sperm donor was being processed and she had talked to Cash again. Of course the only reason she was excited about the latter was that there was a chance he might keep the ranch.

But still, she couldn't ignore the feeling of excitement coursing through her at the thought of seeing him again.

Six

Cash kept telling himself the reason he was excited to be returning to Black Crow had nothing to do with Brianna Banks, and that showing up on Thursday evening instead of Friday morning had nothing to do with the pang of longing he felt whenever he thought about her.

The longing to sample those full, moist lips that had captured him from the first. Or wishing to touch her face, to feel the softness of her skin beneath his fingers. Or wanting the chance to bury his face at the center of her chest to breathe in her scent. He tightened his hands on the steering wheel of the rental car when he saw the marker proclaiming Black Crow's city limits were only ten miles away.

He frowned when his phone rang and he recognized the caller was Maverick. Using the connector on the steering wheel, Cash answered. "What do you want, Maverick?"

"Where are you? I went into your office a few minutes ago and it looked like no-man's-land. Crissy said you checked out for a week."

He'd actually checked out for two weeks, but he figured Maverick would find that out soon enough. "You needed me for something?"

"No, I just wanted to make sure this weekend was still on. I got back to the States last night."

Maverick had jumped at the chance to accompany Sloan to Paris. Sloan was in charge of Outlaw Freight Lines' international sales. Each one of Bart's offspring had a position at the company. Even Jess had been the company's corporate attorney until he'd entered politics to become a senator.

Cash was Garth's right-hand man in the Alaska office, and Maverick's job was overseeing the company's expansion into states like Texas, Florida and the Carolinas. As for Charm… Cash would have to scratch his chin on that one since he and his brothers were still trying to figure out exactly what their sister's duties were. At the moment they'd given her a job mainly to keep her out of their hair.

"How was the trip to Paris?" he asked Maverick.

"What can I say? I love the women there, so what does that tell you?"

Cash shook his head. "I guess you enjoyed yourself."

"Yes, I most certainly did. So now that you've gotten all into my business, answer my question. Where are you?"

"I am on my way to Black Crow to prepare for the weekend." Okay, that would explain why he'd high-tailed it out of Fairbanks a day early, but it wouldn't explain why he'd taken two weeks off. There was no way he would admit to Maverick that he'd been so smitten with Brianna that he wanted two weeks with her to figure out why.

"So, the weekend is still on?"

Hadn't he just said that? Um...did that mean he wasn't the only Outlaw who had allowed some woman to mess with his mind? "Yes, Maverick, but that's something you could have easily asked Sloan."

"I'm not speaking to Sloan."

"Why?"

"Because of his rush to get back to Alaska, I had to cut my time short with Phire."

"Who?"

"You don't know her. I suspect some woman in Fairbanks has caught Sloan's eye. Just like I suspect that woman in Black Crow has caught yours."

Cash decided this was where he changed the subject. "Have you seen or talked to Bart?"

He heard Maverick's chuckle, which meant his youngest brother was fully aware Cash was ready to talk about something else. "Yeah, I saw the old man. He asked where everybody was going this weekend and I told him I wasn't sure. It wasn't a lie since at the time he asked, I wasn't certain if this weekend was still on. Besides, I figure the less Bart knows about your business the better."

"True."

But that hadn't stopped their father from summoning Cash to the Outlaw Estates when he'd returned after the reading of Ellen's will. He had told Bart just enough to satisfy his nosiness. Mainly that Ellen had left him a ranch and the land it was on—all but a hundred acres, which she'd left to a longtime employee. Cash had intentionally mentioned that part because Bart didn't feel any allegiance to employees, longtime or otherwise.

Bart even had the nerve to suggest that Cash contest the will on the grounds that Ellen probably was not in her right mind when it was drawn up, and the woman took advantage of her. Bart felt that as Ellen's son, Cash should have gotten everything.

Cash did not agree with Bart's way of thinking. As nicely and as respectfully as he could, he had told his father to mind his own business.

"At least we don't have to worry about Bart finding out and making a surprise visit," Maverick said.

"And why don't we have to worry about it?" Cash asked, coming to a marker that said Black Crow was only five miles away.

"Because he mentioned Claudia was coming to town this weekend. You know what that means."

Yes, he did. Charm's mother, Claudia, was the one true love of Bart's life. She was also the one woman who had refused to let Bart treat her like the others before her. Bart hadn't known Claudia was pregnant with Charm when their six-month romantic fling had ended, and she had taken off for parts unknown with her daughter.

Fifteen years later, Claudia reappeared with Charm in tow, telling Bart she couldn't handle the sassiness of the daughter he hadn't known he had. She'd given custody to Bart and told him he could deal with it now.

"I assume you'll still be coming, Maverick. If so, I will see you tomorrow."

"Hell, yeah, I'm still coming. I want to check out the woman who has gotten you all in a tizzy."

Cash frowned. "No woman has gotten me in a tizzy."

"If you say so. See you tomorrow, Brother Number Three."

The click sounded loudly in Cash's ear.

Everything looked beautiful, including the fresh flowers in the vases, although Brianna wasn't sure if the men would appreciate the flowers. She was pleased with how things looked and had told Hattie so before she left.

Brianna had walked through every room on both floors. The entire house had a scent that was neither male nor female. It was a robust citrus with hints of lime, oranges, tangelo, lemon and pomelo. It was pleasing.

Going back up the stairs, she rechecked all the bathrooms. She smiled when she saw each had a sufficient number of towels and a basket of toiletries on every vanity that included small canisters of shaving cream and a packet of razors, just in case the men forgot to pack theirs.

She had specifically selected each bedroom so Cash's guests would have a gorgeous view of the mountainous terrain outside their windows.

Although Cash had not given her the time of his arrival tomorrow, she figured it would be before noon. He had said the others would be coming later that evening and he intended to arrive hours before they did. She figured he was coming early to check whether the place was decent. All he had asked her to do was make sure it was suitable to stay for the weekend. She had gone even further and hoped he didn't think she had gone overboard.

Brianna was about to head back downstairs when she caught her reflection in the full-length mirror on the bathroom door. There was no way she could lie and say the reason she had gotten her hair styled and her nails done had anything to do with giving Mrs. Chester, the local hair stylist, her long overdue business. Nor did it have anything to do with Brianna deciding to treat herself. The reason she had pampered herself on a Thursday morning was because of Cash. Although, since she had given him keys to the ranch when she'd given him that tour on Saturday, chances were she wouldn't even see him this weekend. But she wanted to look her best on the slight chance she did.

Heck, for all she knew, he might be bringing his girlfriend, even though he had presented this to her as an all-guys trip. She couldn't see a man who looked like him not being in a serious relationship with someone. If he was, then she wished him the best.

Brianna's ears perked up when she heard a car pull up. Checking her watch, she saw it was five in the afternoon. Had Dano gone grocery shopping today instead of tomorrow? If so, when was he going to let her know? He no longer had a key to the place.

She had taken only a couple steps down the stairs

when the front door swung open. A surprised gasp erupted from her throat when her gaze connected with that of Cash Outlaw.

It took Cash a moment to not only get his bearings but also reclaim his senses. All five of them. Doing so wasn't easy while his gaze was locked on the one woman he had constantly thought about since he'd seen her last. The woman who was the prime reason he had hightailed it out of Fairbanks on a Thursday instead of a Friday. The woman who even from a distance of at least twenty feet could make every single muscle in his body tighten with desire.

"Cash, this is a surprise. I wasn't expecting you until sometime tomorrow," Brianna said, breaking into the passionate haze that seemed to cloud his mind.

Drawing in a deep breath, he responded, "I decided to come up a day early to check on things."

To check on you.

He had seen her car parked outside, and immediately his body had leaped in joy at the thought of seeing her again. He'd honestly thought he would have to come up with some excuse to see her today. Hell, on the way here he'd been trying to come up with one.

"Well, welcome back to the Blazing Frontier."

"Thanks."

Forcing himself to break eye contact with her, he looked around, taking in the changes. The furniture was the same, but the place looked like it had been spruced up a bit. He even noticed the curtains were no longer drawn but were wide open to take full advantage of the sun and the mountain view.

He smiled when he saw the flowers. That was a nice gesture, even if none of the men would truly appreciate them.

Cash then inhaled the citrus scent. It was nice. He switched his gaze back to Brianna and saw she had come down the stairs and now stood only a few feet away. "Everything looks nice, Brianna."

"Thanks. Hattie would be glad to know you are pleased."

"Hattie?"

"Yes, she was over housekeeping here for years. I asked her to come back to get things ready as you requested. And Hattie being Hattie, she couldn't help but go all in."

"I'm glad. It looks nice. I'm sure everyone will appreciate it."

Unable to stop himself, he let his gaze roam over her. Gone was the mane of curls from the last time. Now her hair tumbled in loose waves down her shoulders and he liked it. She looked good in her jeans and peasant blouse.

What hadn't changed was the fact that she was just as captivating as before. He shoved his hands into the pockets of his slacks, figuring that would be the best place for them at the moment. Otherwise, he would be tempted to pull her into his arms and give her the kiss he'd dreamed of since first laying eyes on her.

"*You* look nice, Brianna," he said, giving her the compliment she deserved.

"Thank you, Cash." She paused. "I figured you would prefer using the main bedroom suite. Hattie has made sure it has everything you'll need."

"Thanks."

"And so you won't be surprised when he arrives with the groceries in the morning, Dano, who used to be the head chef, has agreed to be your cook for the weekend."

"That's great."

"I paid both for Hattie's and Dano's services, as well as the rental cost for the additional horses this weekend out of the ranch's contingency fund. I will give you a documented breakdown of everything before you leave on Sunday."

Cash figured now would be a good time to tell her that he wouldn't be leaving on Sunday, that he would be staying for two weeks. Garth had been getting on him for months to take time off. His older brother had reminded Cash that he hadn't taken a real vacation in years.

He had not been able to put up much of an argument because it was the same one he'd given Garth a year or so ago when it seemed his brother was determined to work nonstop, all year round. Now Garth used that same argument against him. He could tell Brianna later about his extended stay, when he saw her again, because he definitely intended to see her again before Sunday.

"I will be leaving to let you get settled," she said, interrupting his thoughts.

She had turned to head for the door when he said, "Have dinner with me, Brianna."

She glanced back at him. "Dinner?"

"Yes, I passed this restaurant on the way here. O'Shea's. It seems like a nice place and I would love if you would join me for dinner. However, if you already have plans, I understand."

Brianna shook her head. "No, I don't have plans. But…"

She was nibbling on her bottom lip in a nervous gesture. He wondered why. "But what?"

"Black Crow is a relatively small town and most people know me. They heard about us sharing a meal before. To do so again would cause speculation."

He lifted a brow. "Is it speculation you prefer not to have for fear your boyfriend might get the wrong idea?"

She rolled her eyes. "Trust me, that's not it because most people know I haven't had a steady boyfriend since…"

"Since what?"

Her chin tightened. "Since I broke up with my last boyfriend."

Now she had him curious. "How long ago was that?"

Surprisingly, Brianna chuckled. "Would you believe since my senior year in high school?"

He definitely found that hard to believe. Was that the same guy who was Roy Dawkins's cousin? She hadn't had a steady boyfriend since high school. Over dinner he intended to find out what was up with that. "I'm not worried about any speculation if you aren't."

"No, I'm not worried. And just so you know, a lot of people are curious about you. You're Ellen's son. A son they didn't know she had."

It was on the tip of his tongue to say, no biggie.

Ellen had conveniently forgotten about him anyway. "I can handle their curiosity, Brianna."

She nodded. "I just wanted to give you fair warning."

"Fair warning taken. Will seven o'clock be okay?"

"Yes, seven will be fine."

"How do I get to your house from here to pick you up?"

"Step out on the porch and I'll show you."

He followed her and recalled she had pointed out where her house was the day they had gone riding together. "It's through those trees there," she said, pointing east.

He had come to stand beside her. Her scent was so alluring he had to breathe in a few times to retain his composure. That really didn't do any good since all he was doing was drawing her scent through his nostrils even more.

"When you turned off the main road, you probably didn't notice the first driveway you came to. Well, it leads to my home. That's one thing I'm going to have to do when you officially sell the place."

"What?"

"Make another entrance to my property so I won't have to drive on Blazing Frontier land to get home."

"I wouldn't worry about it. I'm sure the new owner will be accommodating."

"Maybe they will and maybe they won't." She turned and, as if realizing how close they stood to each other, she took a step back. "You won't miss my house, Cash. It's the only one there. I'll see you at seven."

He watched her move toward the car. She definitely looked good, no matter what she wore.

She turned and said, "I forgot to tell you that I went through some of Ms. Ellen's items in the attic. There was a packet I thought you might want to see, so I placed it in the top drawer of your nightstand."

He was about to tell her she could have thrown it all out as far as he was concerned. Instead he said, "Sure. Thanks."

"You are welcome, Cash."

He loved it when she said his name. There was such a sexy sound to it. Unable to move, he leaned against the wooden post and watched her get into her car to leave.

It was only after she was no longer in sight that he moved to go into the house, where her scent still lingered. Once inside he remembered he needed to get his luggage.

Maverick was right. Brianna did have him in a tizzy.

Seven

Brianna's heart began pounding when she heard a car pull up outside. Glancing out her bedroom window, she saw it was Cash. She leaned against the bedroom door as she tried to regain her composure. She took a deep breath. No matter how drawn she was to him, she couldn't let her attraction get out of hand. Not tonight. Not ever.

One of the first things she needed to master tonight was the ability not to come unglued around him. He had such an overpowering presence that seemed to captivate her every time she was within a few feet of him. She wished he didn't look so handsome or have such a mesmerizing smile.

Brianna had yet to see his frown. It would probably be quite fetching as well. She would have to say the one thing he seemed to have inherited from Ms. Ellen was her pleasing personality.

While getting dressed, she had convinced herself that the only reason she had accepted his invitation to dinner was that she hoped he would share any news regarding the fate of Blazing Frontier.

Giving herself one final check when he knocked, she left her bedroom and moved toward the door. The dress she was wearing was one she had purchased last year when she had gone shopping in Laramie. The saleswoman had convinced her that it flattered her figure. Now, as she looked at herself in it, she would have to agree.

"Who is it?"

"Cash."

She wished he did not have such a sexy-sounding voice. But then, it complemented the rest of his features, she thought, opening the door. He wore a pair of chocolate-brown slacks and a long-sleeve button-up maple-colored shirt. The combination of colors seemed to enhance his appeal.

"Come in. I just need to grab my purse."

She stepped aside and recalled the last man who'd come to visit. Hal Sutherland. But he hadn't made it inside her house. She had talked to him on the porch. That's when he'd told her that after Ms. Ellen died, he would be taking ownership of her home and was giving her notice that she needed to find someplace else to stay. He'd been so certain that he would inherit everything. She was certain he had heard by now that thanks to Ms. Ellen, this house was now hers. He couldn't be happy about that.

Brianna watched Cash glance around when she went to grab her purse off the dining room table. "Nice place," he said.

"Thanks."

"And you look pretty."

"Thanks again, and I'm ready to leave." The sooner they got out of her house the better. He was no taller than her dad had been, yet Cash's presence seemed to make the house shrink in size.

"I hope you're hungry because I definitely am. I could eat a horse," he said when they walked to the car.

Brianna glanced over at him and smiled. She had noticed that day at lunch that he had a healthy appetite. Very few people could eat two of Monroe's hamburgers, but he had.

"I'm hungry but I won't be eating a horse, Cash. Neither will you. O'Shea's has the juiciest steaks in southeast Wyoming and the most delicious sides to go along with them. You get to select three instead of two."

"Sounds like my kind of place. What about desserts?"

She glanced at him when he opened the car door for her. "If you like peaches then you'd love their cobbler. Their butter pound cake isn't bad either. The reason O'Shea's is so popular is that it has a great atmosphere and the food is wonderful."

A short while later, when she and Cash entered the restaurant, it seemed everyone was focused on them. She was glad they were shown to a table that overlooked the river. The waitress gave them a minute to look at the menus.

"What river is that?" he asked, gesturing to the window. It hadn't gotten dark yet and boaters were still out.

"That's the Keystone River."

"The same one on our properties?"

Our properties.

She knew he hadn't meant it the way he'd said it, but yes, it was the same one on *their* properties since they now shared a part of Keystone River.

"Yes. The Keystone River is enormous and is somewhat in the shape of a huge S. The curve encompasses our properties and Hal Sutherland's land. The tip at the top feeds into the Arrowhead River in Cheyenne."

The waitress returned to take their order and bring their drinks. Cash had ordered a bottle of wine for the table, one she had suggested. She watched as he took his first sip and when he licked his lips, she felt a stirring in her midsection.

"Well, what do you think, Cash?"

He glanced over at her and smiled. "I like it."

She was glad. "Are you ready for this weekend?" she asked, hoping if she got him talking about it, he would give her a clue as to his plans for the ranch.

"Yes. It's always a grand time when my brothers, cousins and I get together. Now I have a question for you."

She lifted a brow. "What question is that?"

He met her gaze and asked, "Why haven't you had a steady guy in your life since high school?"

From Brianna's expression, Cash knew she was surprised by his question. Of course, she had every right to tell him it wasn't any of his business, but since she'd been the one to let it slip earlier, he was merely appeasing his curiosity.

She held his gaze, and for a quick moment he saw a flash of pain in the depths of her eyes. Seeing it should have extinguished his curiosity, but instead it made him want to know that much more. What had happened to her in high school that still affected her now?

"Alan Dawkins and I dated all through high school."

"Dawkins? Is he related to Roy? The guy who owns the clothing store?" he asked, wanting to confirm what the man had told him.

"Yes, Roy is Alan's cousin. Anyway, Alan graduated from high school a year ahead of me. Our plans were for him to go into the army, and then we would marry the next year when I graduated."

"What happened to him?" Cash asked. Did the man lose his life while in the military? That's what had happened to Garth's fiancée Karen. It had taken years before his brother had gotten over losing her. Everyone was glad when Garth had fallen in love with Regan.

"Germany happened. While stationed over there, he met someone, fell in love and married her. End of story."

Not quite, he quickly decided. He was certain the decent thing to do was to let it go, but for some reason, he could not. "He came home married to someone else?"

She hesitated and then said, "Yes."

Cash took another sip of his wine. He could just imagine a younger Brianna, excited about finishing high school while planning a wedding, only to find out the man she loved, a man she thought loved her, had committed his life to someone else.

"I'm sorry that happened to you, Brianna," he said in a quiet tone, truly meaning it.

"Thanks." She took a sip of her own wine. "That was years ago. Close to ten, in fact, and I've gotten over it."

He leaned back in his chair. "If that's true, then why aren't you in a serious relationship now?"

She shrugged. "I only have one heart. It's been broken once, and it took me a while to repair it. I don't want it broken again."

He nodded. "You don't ever plan to give love another chance?"

"I can't see it happening."

He didn't say anything for a moment. "I think that's really sad, Brianna. In the short time I've gotten to know you, I think you're a nice woman who has a lot to offer someone."

It was kind of Cash to say that. "Thank you."

Thinking it was fair to change the subject to what *she* wanted to know, she said, "Now it's my time to ask you a question."

They paused when the waitress came with their food. It smelled delicious and she hoped Cash thought it tasted delicious as well. "What question is that?" he asked after the waitress had left and he was reaching for the steak sauce.

She watched as he poured sauce on his meat. "Is there a reason for this weekend?"

He lifted his head and looked at her. "If you're asking if inviting my family and friends means I'm no longer thinking about selling the ranch, then the answer is no. That still remains an option I am considering."

"Oh."

"However, I will say that my brothers think selling the ranch might be a mistake."

"They do?" She couldn't keep the excitement out of her voice.

He smiled. "Yes. That's the reason they want to come check it out. They also suggested it could become a horse ranch, which is why my cousins are coming. They are in the horse breeding and training business. And then there are a few in my family who believe I can have horses and a dude ranch."

Brianna nodded. She could definitely see any of those options working. In fact, the horse business could benefit the dude ranch. "I think having both a dude ranch and a horse ranch would be wonderful. It would certainly boost the economy around here again."

"We'll see."

Brianna decided not to push the issue. She just hoped whatever plan he came up with would be one in which he would retain control of the ranch and not sell it. Ellen would have wanted that. It made her wonder—had he gone through the packet she had left in the drawer in his bedroom? Obviously not, since he hadn't mentioned it.

Before she could ask him about it, a deep male voice spoke. It was a voice she recognized, and it made her cringe. "Cashen Outlaw, right?"

Cash glanced up at the man who had approached

their table. He stood when the man extended his hand. "Yes, I'm Cashen Outlaw."

"I'm Hal Sutherland," the man said, smiling broadly. "I spoke with you last week about buying the Blazing Frontier."

"Yes, I recall that you did." Cash looked at Brianna and then back at Hal. "I'm sure you know Brianna Banks, right?"

Hal barely gave her a cursory nod. "Brianna."

"Hal." Brianna knew he would have ignored her if Cash had not forced him to acknowledge her presence.

Hal glanced back at Cash. "So, when can we meet to talk business?"

"I haven't made any decisions about what I plan to do."

Brianna could tell from the look on Hal's face that he found Cash's words surprising as well as disappointing.

"Why would you want to keep it?" Hal asked as if he had every right to know.

Cash smiled. "For a number of reasons. Now, if you don't mind, Brianna and I want to finish our meal before it gets cold." He sat back down.

"Oh. Okay. Sure." Hal then walked off.

Brianna glanced over at Cash. "That doesn't happen often," she said.

"What?" Cash asked while cutting into his steak.

"Hal getting dismissed by anyone."

Cash shrugged. "There's a first time for everything."

"Thanks for joining me for dinner, Brianna. And you were right. The food was delicious," Cash said when they walked up the steps to her home.

"Thanks for inviting me. I'm glad you enjoyed everything."

"It's a beautiful night," he said, looking up into the sky while leaning against a porch post.

Brianna followed his gaze. "Yes, it is. We don't have the northern lights like Alaska, but I think a Wyoming sky is simply beautiful."

Cash looked over at her. She was beautiful, too. It had been a wonderful night and he had enjoyed sharing it with her. "Speaking of tonight, as nice as it was, there is one thing that I didn't appreciate."

She glanced over at him. "Oh? What?"

"Hal Sutherland interrupting our dinner." He paused. "I picked up on tension between the two of you. Is there something I should know?"

He watched her nibble on her bottom lip, something that happened whenever he crossed unpleasant waters with her. His protective instincts went up. It bothered him that anything or anyone could upset her.

"Hal was Mr. Van's nephew, and Blazing Frontier was part of their family spread. Mr. Van and his first wife never had children, and everyone, including Hal, assumed if anything ever happened to Mr. Van, the ranch would belong to Hal as his heir."

"Um, let me guess," Cash said. "Mr. Van married Ellen and changed the dynamics."

"Yes. And while Mr. Van was alive, Hal pretty much behaved himself. The minute Mr. Van died, Hal approached Ellen and made her an offer to buy the property, assuming she would sell and move back east. She surprised him when she turned him down. He didn't like it much and caused problems, trying to force her to sell. She didn't." She paused. "He figured you had no reason to want to keep the land and would be glad to accept his offer."

Why did Cash have a feeling there was more? "And what else, Brianna?"

Brianna glanced down at the porch's floor and didn't say anything for a long moment before looking back up at him. "There's nothing else, Cash. At least, not anymore. Hal made it known that if he ever became the owner of the Blazing Frontier, one of the first things he would do would be to evict me from my home."

Cash raised a brow. "Why?"

"Hal is a man who holds grudges. He believes my parents are the reason Ms. Ellen didn't sell the ranch to him when Mr. Van died. Since my parents are no longer alive, he has extended his grudge to me."

"That's crazy."

She shrugged. "It doesn't matter now. Even if you were to sell the ranch to him, thanks to Ms. Ellen, this house and the acres it sits on are mine, and there is nothing he can do about it."

Hearing the strong emotion in her words made Cash glad that Ellen had done that for her. With a life of their own, his hands reached out and gently caressed her face. "I'm glad, Brianna."

Their gazes held and then he felt it—what he felt whenever he was around her. Sexual chemistry. It was stronger than ever tonight. He watched as she slowly drew in a deep breath, and as if they were a magnet, his lips were drawn closer.

His mouth unerringly went to hers. Tasting her was what he needed. This was what he had been thinking of doing since the day he had seen her licking that ice-cream cone. Now he was licking her, and he almost felt weak in the knees when she began licking him back.

Cash hadn't counted on the rush of heated desire that invaded his loins the moment their tongues connected. Nor had he counted on bone-melting fire spreading right into his soul. He began devouring her mouth in a way that should have been outlawed. It was as deep as you could take a kiss, his tongue boldly dueling with hers.

He tasted the pure sweetness of her mouth, and when he deepened the kiss, he couldn't help the moan forced from his throat. She leaned into him, her soft body pressing against his hard one. The sexual chemistry between them was out of control, at a level he had never encountered or expected. His testosterone level had never been revved up this much. But it had reached its boiling point, just for her.

The ringing of his cell phone had him dragging his mouth away from Brianna's. He recognized the ringtone. Charm. He would call her back later. For now, he wanted to pull Brianna back into his arms and kiss her again. He reached out for her, but she took a step back.

"I better get inside now," she said in a rush. "I hope you and your family enjoy your weekend. Good night, Cash." She turned to open the door.

"Wait. There's something I need to ask you."

She turned back around. "What?"

Cash studied her wet and swollen lips and felt a sense of gratification that he had done that. "Would you come to the ranch house tomorrow for dinner? I met Dano when he delivered the groceries today instead of waiting until tomorrow, and he says he's preparing a feast. I expect everyone to have arrived by four, and dinner will be served at seven. I'd like my family to meet you."

She raised a surprised brow. "Why would you want that?"

He really couldn't tell her why. All he knew was that he wanted to see her again and wanted his family to meet her. He decided to come up with a plausible reason. "Because you obviously meant a lot to Ellen. And I'm hoping if you're free on Saturday, you'll agree to be our tour guide. I know it's short notice, and if you have other plans I understand. You know every inch of Blazing Frontier and would do a better job showing everyone around than I could."

She didn't say anything as she studied the porch's floor again. Finally, she lifted her gaze to him. "I would love to join you for dinner tomorrow and meet your family. And I don't have anything planned on Saturday, if you think I'm really needed."

He smiled. "Yes, you'll be needed."

Whether she knew it or not, that kiss was just the beginning.

She nodded. "Good night, Cash."

Cash wasn't ready for the night to end. He was tempted to pull her into his arms again. Give her another kiss. Instead he knew he had to let her go. Besides, he needed to figure out why Brianna Banks had gotten under his skin in a way no other woman had before.

"Good night, Brianna. You were the perfect date."

* * *

You were the perfect date...

Cash's words floated through Brianna's mind as she stood by her living room window and watched the lights from his car fade into black. She honestly hadn't thought of it as a date until he'd said it. But now she concurred. After all, he had asked her out, picked her up, taken her to dinner and made sure she enjoyed herself.

And then he gave me one unforgettable good-night kiss.

She touched her lips, still tingling from his kiss. She had never been kissed like that before. Not for a good-night kiss or any other kind. He had taken her mouth like he owned every inch of it, searing her insides with passion.

She moved away from the window and sighed deeply. Her heart beat furiously in her chest. She needed to get a grip. Just because he had invited her to share his weekend didn't necessarily mean a thing. If nothing else, Alan had taught her to only believe in herself and no one else.

But still, there were so many things about Cash that she liked. And for someone who had been prepared not to like him, that said a lot. What really impressed her tonight was his handling of Hal. Although Hal wasn't all that liked around town, people knew not to cross him. Her parents, Mr. Van and Ms. Ellen had been some of the few who had stood up to him. Now she could add Cash to that list. Tonight, he had proven that he was not a man to take lightly. She had a feeling Hal realized that.

As she moved around the bedroom to undress, her spirits were soaring too high to think about going to sleep. She checked her watch. Miesha was a late-nighter and Brianna picked up her phone to call her friend.

"Hello."

"Guess what I did tonight, Miesha."

"Had sex with some hunk with enough orgasms for the both of us?"

Brianna couldn't help but scream in laughter. Her friend could say some of the most outlandish things at times. "No, I didn't have sex, but I did have a date."

"Do tell. You're glowing all the way through the phone."

Brianna figured that could be true because she felt giddy inside. When had a date ever left her feeling that way? "Cash Outlaw returned to town today and asked me out."

"I thought you said he wouldn't be coming back."

"I honestly thought he wouldn't, but he called and said he would be coming back for the weekend." Brianna then told her friend everything, ending with the whopper of a kiss on her porch.

"Hey, I like this Cash Outlaw. And for him to invite you for dinner to meet his family means something."

Brianna rolled her eyes. "It means he appreciates me agreeing to take his family on a tour Saturday."

"I don't see it that way. I've been around more men than you, so I know how they operate. You gave him a tour of the ranch last week, right?"

"Right."

"Then he should be capable of showing everyone

around on his own. It shouldn't be that complicated. You know what I think?"

Brianna smiled. "No, what do you think?"

"I think he is using the tour as an excuse to spend time with you. He obviously likes you and that might be a good thing."

"How so?"

"If you decide not to use an unknown donor's sperm, you might want to place him at the top of the list."

Brianna's jaw almost dropped. "You've got to be kidding."

"Why would I kid about something like that? If you ask him, all he can do is say yes or no, Brianna."

"And he would say no, trust me."

"You can't be certain of that. I think it's a wonderful idea, and if you let him know you'll take full responsibility for raising your son, Cash just might be fine with it."

"Yes, but I'm not sure I would be."

"I don't see why not. You thought the world of Ms. Ellen and she thought the world of you. It makes perfect sense to me that you would be the mother of her grandchild."

Brianna didn't say anything for a moment, refusing to let Miesha fill her head with crazy thoughts. "For all I know, Cash Outlaw might be in a relationship."

"Not if he kissed you the way you said he did tonight. I'm not saying he doesn't date, because he probably does. That's not the same as a relationship. Besides, he will let you know if he's unavailable when you broach the subject of fathering your child."

Brianna shook her head. "No, I can't do that. It won't work."

"Okay, it was just a suggestion."

A short while later, after hanging up the phone with Miesha, Brianna began getting ready for bed. After-effects from that kiss were still thrumming through her body and a part of her couldn't wait to see Cash again tomorrow.

However, she could not and would not entertain the thought of Cash Outlaw fathering her child—no matter how appealing the idea might be.

Eight

"This is one hell of a nice place, Cash," Garth said as he stood on the porch and looked out over the land. "I can't wait for the tour tomorrow."

Cash smiled as he handed his oldest brother a bottle of beer. Garth had been the last to arrive. Now all his houseguests were accounted for. Most were in the saloon and the others were at the game center, shooting pool. Like Garth, everyone had been taken with the place.

"Hopefully, you'll know by the end of the weekend what you plan to do with it."

"Yes, I should know by then." Cash paused. "Can I ask you something, Garth?"

"Yes, what?"

"It's about Karen."

For years, the family had known never to mention

the woman Garth had loved who'd died in a copter accident, because whenever they did, they saw the pain in their brother's eyes. But now Garth had moved on with his life. He was married to Regan and the spark was back in his eyes.

Garth lifted a brow. "What about Karen?"

"I recall you saying that from the first time you met her, you knew she was special."

Garth studied his brother as he took another swig of beer. "I did. That's not saying I hadn't dated women I thought were special before. I just knew there was something different about her. I knew she was the one." He leaned against the porch rail. "Have you met such a woman, Cash?"

Cash met his brother's gaze and nodded. "I think I have."

"Brianna Banks?"

Cash didn't say anything for a minute and then, "Yes."

Garth nodded. "Is that why you're taking two weeks off to hang around here? Not that I don't think you deserve the time off."

"I'm not going to say she's the only reason, but I'd be fooling myself to think she doesn't have a lot to do with it."

"Then you're doing the right thing. Hindsight is twenty-twenty. Regan said she'd been in love with me for years. And when I think of the time I could have spent with her being as happy as I am now, I see them as wasted years, Cash. Life is too short to live it with regrets." He paused again. "I think even Bart has regrets."

"You think so?"

Garth smiled. "Maybe not with any of our mothers, but definitely with Charm's. If he could marry Claudia today, he would."

"You think he's learned his lesson?"

"No. Claudia probably does not think he has either, which is why she won't marry him. I honestly don't think he'll ever change. He might be a different person around her, but on the inside he's still the same Bart."

Cash didn't say anything as he took a swallow of his own beer. Then he said, "I invited her to dinner."

"Who?"

"Brianna."

Garth smiled. "I can't wait to meet her."

Brianna saw all the vehicles parked in front of the ranch house the moment she turned in to the driveway. She tried to calm the butterflies in her stomach, telling herself she didn't have a reason to be nervous. Although she didn't know any of Cash's guests, she did know him.

She parked behind a truck, got out of the car and glanced down at herself. She would be looking like a cowgirl tomorrow when she took them on the tour. Today she had dressed up in her long, flowing maxi skirt with a long-sleeve blouse and boots. Her favorite necklace, a gift from her parents on her twenty-first birthday, was around her neck, and the matching earrings were in her ears.

She had taken one step toward the door when it opened and Cash stepped out. If she didn't know better, she would think he'd been waiting for her, but she did know better. "Hello, Cash."

He smiled at her. "Hello, Brianna. You look very nice."

"Thanks."

"Everyone is in the dining room."

"Alright."

He surprised her by taking her hand, something he hadn't done last night. She walked with him toward the dining room, taking time to wave at Dano. She heard loud voices and the butterflies appeared again. Right before she entered the dining room, Cash said, "Thanks for coming."

She smiled up at him. "Thanks for inviting me."

Tightening his hand on hers, he then led her to where several guys were talking. "We have a guest for dinner," Cash said loudly to get their attention.

It seemed all eyes turned their way, giving her curious stares. She figured more so because Cash hadn't let go of her hand. "Guys, I'd like you to meet a friend, Brianna Banks. She and her parents used to work here at the ranch. Brianna will be our tour guide tomorrow."

He then said to her, "Come on, let me take you around to introduce you to everyone. I don't expect you to remember them by name, though."

First, he introduced her to his brothers, Garth, Jess, Sloan and Maverick. It didn't take long for her to see that Cash's youngest brother, Maverick, was a natural born flirt who enjoyed rattling Cash. Jess was a United States Senator who made his home in the nation's capital. Garth and Jess were older than Cash, and Sloan and Maverick were younger. She could feel a closeness between the brothers. They told her about their sister, Charm, who was a couple years younger than Brianna.

Then he introduced her to his Westmoreland cousins—Zane, Derringer, Jason, Durango, Clint and Bane. There was a striking resemblance between the Outlaw brothers and their Westmoreland cousins. It was uncanny how much Cash and Bane favored. The only difference was their eye coloring. Bane had hazel eyes. However, unless she was standing right in front of them, she wouldn't notice the difference.

Then there were two friends of the Westmorelands, Bane's navy SEAL teammates—Laramie Cooper, who everyone called Coop, and Thurston McRoy, who was called Mac. The two men also owned horse ranches and while away on missions hired trusted foremen to run their spreads. Last, she was introduced to McKinnon Quinn, cousin-in-law of the Westmorelands, who was married to Clint Westmoreland's sister. McKinnon was gorgeous with thick black hair that fell to his shoulders. He told her he was Blackfoot Indian and African American Creole. He and Durango lived in Montana and were the two who had started the horse training and breeding business.

"I can't believe how much the Outlaws and the Westmorelands favor. Especially you and Bane," Brianna told Cash when he seated her beside him at the long table.

He smiled over at her. "Remind me to tell you how I switched places with Bane once, to help bring down a group of bad guys who were threatening his wife."

Brianna lifted a brow. "You're serious?"

He smiled. "Yes, I'm serious."

She enjoyed dining with everyone and although she was the only female in the group, she in no way felt left out of the conversation. These guys were ranchers and she was familiar with a lot of their topics and even added her two cents, especially when they began discussing horses. She could tell they were surprised and impressed with her knowledge.

"How do you know so much about horse ranching? Cash said you worked as the manager of the dude ranch," Clint Westmoreland said, smiling over at her.

"I did, but I was also the daughter of a lifelong foreman. Specifically of this ranch. I grew up here and remember when it was a cattle ranch and there were plenty of horses. I have a barn at my place and keep three horses there and care for them myself."

Dano had outdone himself with dinner and everyone was singing the chef's praises while enjoying the dessert he'd prepared—peach cobbler with what some of the guys claimed was the best coffee they'd ever had.

Every man here was handsome as sin. And she was surprised to learn that they were all married except for Cash's brothers Jess, Sloan and Maverick. Some of the guys and their wives had multiple births…something Cash said was common in his family. Bane was the father of triplets, and Jason and Mac were the fathers of twins. She'd also discovered Clint was part of triplets. He had a brother named Cole, and his sister Casey was married to McKinnon. Bane's triplets were Ace, Adam and Anna Clarisse. Bane's brother Jason had twin girls, one of whom was named Clarisse Hope. Jason and Bane explained they had both wanted to give their mother's name, Clarisse, to their daughters. Brianna thought it was a touching gesture.

When it was time to leave, she stood and said to the group, "I'm looking forward to showing all of you around tomorrow."

"And we're looking forward to having you as our tour guide," Maverick said, smiling and winking at her.

Cash insisted that he follow Brianna back home to make sure she got there safely, although she had told him that wasn't necessary. It was to him.

He parked his car beside hers and got out to walk her up to the door. "So, what do you think of the Outlaws, Westmorelands and friends?"

She smiled up at him when they reached her door. "The guys are wonderful and I like how they are family men. They love their wives and children."

He lifted a brow. "Isn't that the way it's supposed to be?"

"Yes, but it's not always. I was blessed to have parents who loved each other and who loved me, and the same thing with the kids I grew up with. When I got to college, I discovered that wasn't always the case. My best friend's mom has been married three times and her father, four."

"My father, Bart, has them beat," Cash said. "He's been married and divorced five times and had a son by each of the women. Me and my brothers have different mothers."

"Yet all of you get along."

He chuckled. "No reason we shouldn't. Our father, Bart, raised the five of us and wasn't keen on us having friends. Except for Walker Rafferty. He's been Garth's best friend since they were babies. And Regan, who's married to Garth now. She grew up around us since her father was the corporate pilot for Outlaw Freight Lines for over forty years."

"What about your sister, Charm? Who is her mother?"

Cash was surprised how comfortable he felt discussing his family with Brianna, something he barely did with anyone. "Bart was never married to Charm's mother, and but we know that is something he regrets and would undo if he could. That's a whole other story."

"Thanks for seeing me safely home. Although you really didn't have to, I appreciate it."

He smiled down at her. "Do you appreciate it enough to invite me in for coffee?"

"What about your guests?"

"What about them? Last time I looked they were grown-ass men who can fend for themselves. Besides, a third of them are going to return to playing pool, a third will find their way over to the saloon, and the other third will hang near the kitchen for a second helping of Dano's pie and coffee. Everything was delicious. Thanks for setting up this weekend."

"You're welcome. Do you honestly want a cup of coffee?"

"Yes." He would tell her later he wanted a kiss as well, but he didn't want to do it out here on her porch like he had last night.

"Then a cup of coffee it is," she said, opening the door.

When they were inside and he closed the door behind him, she said, "Make yourself at home and when I return with our coffee, I want to hear all about the time you switched places with Bane to protect his wife."

He chuckled. "Okay."

Cash watched her disappear into her kitchen and went over to her fireplace to look at the framed photographs sitting on the mantel. He figured the older couple was her parents and smiled at her graduation photo.

He recalled what she had told him at dinner last night. Her boyfriend, who was supposed to return to marry her when she graduated, had married someone else. His betrayal was the reason she could never give her heart to another man. Cash could just imagine not only the hurt she'd had to endure but also the embarrassment when he returned with his wife. In a small town like Black Crow, that must have been humiliating. She hadn't deserved that. The guy hadn't deserved her.

Music began playing and Cash immediately recognized the song and the artist. "I'm back," she said, carrying a tray with two cups of coffee. Setting the tray on the coffee table, she handed him a cup.

"Thanks. I take it you like Dylan Emanuel's music."

"I love it. He's a gifted musician and he has such a way with words. And his voice is superb. He's up for another Grammy this year."

"So I heard. I met him once."

Her eyes widened. "You did?"

"Yes. It was years ago. He was seventeen and had won a summer scholarship to attend the University of Alaska's Fairbanks Summer Music Academy. My sister, Charm, had the chance to get to know Dylan when one of her piano instructors also taught Dylan that summer."

There was no need to tell Brianna how Bart had found out about the budding romance between Charm and Dylan and hadn't wasted any time putting an end to what Bart had called utter teenage nonsense.

Brianna eased down on the sofa, tucking her legs beneath her as she stirred her coffee. "Your sister plays the piano?"

He shook his head, grinning. "No. She bummed out on those lessons." He took a sip of coffee. "There is nothing like good coffee. It's delicious."

She smiled. "Thanks. I can't compete with Dano, but I don't do so bad. Dad taught me. He said, 'Don't mess around when it comes to a cowboy's coffee.'"

"Well, I like it. And you know what else I like, Brianna?"

"No. What?"

"Seeing you smile. You have a beautiful smile."

"Flattery is nice, but don't think it's going to get you out of telling me what I want to know, Cash," she said, grinning. "Now, tell me about the time you and Bane traded places."

He couldn't help but laugh. "Okay, here goes."

He spent the next twenty minutes telling her the story. He felt okay in doing so since it had made news when Homeland Security had arrested all those involved.

"Wow! That's just like reading a spy novel. I'm glad Bane and his wife were okay."

"I am, too, but it was never Bane and Crystal who were really in danger. It was those men who thought they could actually take her away from Bane. My family believes in protecting what's theirs."

Brianna nodded. "The one thing I noticed about your family is that they are close. Must be nice."

"It is, especially since the Outlaws and Westmorelands only discovered they were related a few years ago."

She lifted a brow. "You're kidding. How? Why?"

Cash then told her how the Outlaws and Westmorelands discovered they were related. He also mentioned how Garth's best friend, Walker Rafferty, had visited the Westmorelands in Denver to verify the kinship. Walker had met Bailey Westmoreland, the two had fallen in love and ended up marrying. "So there you have it," he said when he finished the story.

"That's way too much action for me," she said, shaking her head. The gesture made a few curls dance around her shoulders.

He wanted to touch those curls, but instead he glanced at his watch and stood. "It's getting late and you need your sleep."

She stood as well and chuckled. "I need my sleep?"

"Yes, we're heading out at dawn, remember?"

"Yes, I remember, and I'll be fine. Baby and I love going out riding that time of morning."

"Baby?"

"Yes, my horse. I'll ride Baby over to your place."

"Okay," he said, following her as she led him to the door.

Upon reaching it, she turned to him. "Thanks again for making sure I got home safely and sharing your family with me, Cash."

He took a step closer to her and gave in to the need to push a strand of hair from her face. "You are welcome."

Then he lowered his mouth to hers for the kiss he so desperately needed. The kiss he'd spent most of the night anticipating. The kiss he had gotten addicted to last night.

Everything about her kiss pleased him. The moment she wrapped her arms around his neck, he deepened the kiss. She moaned, and he loved the sound. He loved the feel of her body plastered to his. He greedily took her mouth like it would be his last chance to do so.

Although he wished otherwise, he knew he couldn't stand here and kiss her all night. Slowly and reluctantly, he ended the kiss. But not before sweeping her lips with his tongue.

"I love kissing you," he said against her moist lips. "The first time I saw your mouth, I got turned on by it. Do you know when that was?"

She smiled up at him. "In Mr. Cavanaugh's office?"

"No. Before that."

Her forehead bunched up. "Before Mr. Cavanaugh's office?"

"Yes."

"But I hadn't met you before then."

"True, but I had seen you. The moment I entered town. I was stopped at a traffic light and saw you coming out of an ice-cream shop. Seeing how you were licking that ice-cream cone made my entire body ache."

She didn't say anything. In fact, she actually blushed, and he thought it was the cutest thing. Not able to help himself, he leaned down and kissed her again.

Moments later, he slowly pulled back, flicked his gaze over her features and saw the expression of a satisfied woman. He smiled, knowing he'd done that. "Good night, Brianna. I'll see you in the morning."

"Baby and I will be there."

He couldn't wait to see the mare she called Baby. He then opened the door. If he didn't leave now, he would be tempted to kiss her yet again.

Nine

"Will you look at that beauty of a horse Brianna is riding?" Zane Westmoreland remarked, staring off in the distance.

Cash turned and like the others, stared at horse and rider. He knew the others were checking out the horse. He was checking out the rider. She looked absolutely stunning galloping across the plains toward them. The mass of hair beneath her wide-brimmed hat was flying in the wind while she sat astride a huge white stallion that looked fierce. Like he could eat you alive. That was Baby?

Cash chuckled, deciding the joke was on him. Baby was not a docile mare like he'd assumed. Zane was right. It was a beauty of a horse. And Brianna was handling him like a pro. He glanced around and saw admiration and respect in his family's and friends' eyes.

"Good morning, guys. You ready?" she asked when she came to a stop in front of them.

"Good morning. Yes, we're ready," Cash said, smiling over at her. "That's a beautiful horse."

"Thanks. Baby has been mine since he was a colt."

"Baby?" Durango Westmoreland said, chuckling. "He doesn't look like a baby. He looks mean."

"He can be to others but not to me. He's very protective of me."

"You handle him well," Clint Westmoreland said.

"Thanks." She smiled at everyone. "By the way, Dano will have lunch ready for us in the lower valley of your property at noon."

Cash lifted a brow. "He will?"

"Yes, that will save us time since we won't need to return to the ranch house."

Cash was glad she had thought of that and taken care of the arrangements. "Where are we headed to first?"

"The range. I want everyone to see how vast it is."

"Then lead the way."

Nearly five hours later, Cash would admit everyone was enjoying themselves. His Denver Westmoreland cousins indicated their land lacked the valleys and plains here, and that the only time they could ride this freely was when they visited Clint's spread in Austin. Everyone was surprised when at noon they returned to the spot where lunch would be served. Dano had a barbecue pit going and had set up tables to accommodate everyone. The meal had been served with baked beans, potato salad and the best-tasting punch. The weather was perfect.

Right before dusk, everyone returned to the ranch, tired and excited about how the day had gone. The guys thanked Brianna for being a great tour guide and told her goodbye since they wouldn't see her again before leaving tomorrow. They then headed inside to shower after what they all considered a wonderful day spent out on the range.

Cash held back to again talk to Brianna before she rode off for home. She was sitting astride Baby and he stood beside her, glancing up. "Everyone enjoyed themselves, Brianna. I could tell they were impressed with the place."

Her smile widened. "I'm glad. It was good seeing you again this weekend, Cash. I hope all of you have a safe trip back home." Then, as if on impulse, she leaned down and swiped a quick kiss across his lips.

Before he could react, she straightened in the saddle and took off. She and Baby went racing across the yard toward her home. He licked his lips, still tasting her there.

He'd never got around to telling her that he would be staying for two weeks. He grinned. She would find out soon enough.

"So, what do you guys think?" Cash asked the crew around the table later that evening.

It was McKinnon who answered. "You are sitting on a gold mine. This place is perfect for a horse ranch. I can also see you turning it back into a dude ranch. You have enough land to do both. There is one thing I suggest you do, though."

"What?" Cash asked.

"I heard you mention to Zane that you don't have full access to Keystone River from your property."

"That's right. I share it with someone," Cash replied.

"I suggest you contact the owner and make them an offer for it. That could not only be beneficial in a number of ways, but perhaps also necessary."

Cash lifted a brow. "Why?"

"The more water you have for the horses, the better, especially during the year when the water holes on the property become dry. I did my research and that has happened in this area a few times."

"Do you know the person you share that property with? Do you think they would be interested in selling the land?" Bane asked.

Cash didn't say anything. "Yes, I know the owner. In fact, the land was part of the original deed to the ranch before Ellen died."

"Then what happened?"

Cash rubbed his hand down his face before saying, "Ellen divided it up in her will. That part of the property was given to Brianna."

Derringer smiled. "Oh, well, then you don't have anything to worry about. She might just sell it back to you or at the very least, let you lease the land."

"I'd prefer if he made an offer to buy it," Durango said. "McKinnon and I tried leasing land to expand and ran into problems. When it came time to renew the lease, the landowner doubled the price because he knew how essential the land was to our business."

"I can't see Brianna ever doing something like that," Sloan said. It was obvious Sloan had been taken with Brianna.

"Probably not Brianna, but she's young and single. What if she marries one day and her husband is an ass with a lot of influence on her?"

"Brianna can't up and marry anybody," Maverick said matter-of-factly, grinning from ear to ear.

"Why not?" Mac was curious to know.

"Because she's Cash's girl. Didn't you see how he was practically breathing down her neck all weekend? Even on Friday night, his hand seemed to be glued to hers."

Zane rubbed his chin. "Yes, I noticed. I think we all did." He then glanced over at Cash. "Is she your girl?"

Cash found it somewhat amusing how they had been discussing him like he hadn't been in their presence. When he didn't answer right away, an impatient Sloan asked, "Well, is she your girl or not, Cash?"

Cash gave his brother a slow smile. "Yes, Brianna is my girl. She's all mine."

It was strange that he'd just done something he'd never thought he would. Claim a woman as his. But he felt damn good about it, even though he didn't know how Brianna might feel about him stating ownership the way he just had. She had no idea that he wanted to engage in a relationship with her—not just to see where it went, but to make sure it went where he wanted it to go.

Cash then remembered what she'd told him about never wanting to fall in love again for fear of having her heart broken. She'd seemed pretty damn adamant about it. That meant he had to come up with a plan to win Brianna over.

And he would.

Ten

Brianna was surprised when she arrived at the Blazing Frontier bright and early Monday morning to find Cash's rental car still parked in the driveway. Did he not leave with the others yesterday? She didn't recall him saying he would stay longer.

She tried to stop her heart from beating so rapidly as she got out of the car, not sure why she was so anxious when she'd been around Cash all weekend. But then, there had been others around as well. Now they would be alone and the last couple times they'd been alone, he had kissed her. Would he do so again? Did she want him to?

She walked up the steps and before she could knock, the door opened.

"Good morning, Brianna," Cash said, smiling at her.

She tried to ignore the effect that smile had on her.

"I thought you would be leaving with the others," she said, walking into the ranch house when he moved aside.

"I decided to stay awhile."

"Oh."

"I looked forward to seeing you this morning," he said.

"How did you know I was coming over today?"

"Dano mentioned you would be returning to go through Ellen's belongings. I was just about to grab a cup of coffee and some of those strawberry muffins Dano made. Will you join me?"

Brianna figured there was no reason she shouldn't. Besides, maybe he would tell her if he had made a decision about the ranch. "I'd love to join you," she said, following him into the kitchen. He looked good in his jeans and shirt. "Why did you decide to remain here instead of leaving with the others yesterday?" she asked before she could stop herself from doing so.

When he turned and looked at her over his shoulder, she quickly added, "Sorry, it's really not any of my business."

He pulled two cups out of the cabinet and poured coffee into them. "In a way, it is your business. I decided to help you go through Ellen's things after all."

The pulse beat in her neck. "You have?"

"Yes."

She met his gaze when he handed her the coffee. What had made him change his mind? Had he gotten around to seeing that packet she had left in his bedroom? Whatever the reason, she didn't want to think about them being in such close proximity.

"How long will you be staying?"

He met her gaze. "That depends on you."

"On me?" she asked, surprised.

"Yes. I plan to be here for as long as you need me here."

She nodded. They were still talking about working together to go through Ellen's things, right? Brianna took a sip of her coffee and tried not to think of him possibly meaning anything else.

Deciding to change the subject, she asked, "Did everyone enjoy themselves this weekend?"

"Yes, they did. They were impressed with the place," he said, setting a plate of muffins in front of her. He had warmed them up and they smelled heavenly.

"Blazing Frontier is a beautiful spread," she said before taking a bite. She glanced up and saw him staring at her. She licked a crumb off her bottom lip and then asked, "Is anything wrong?"

He shook his head and smiled. "No, there's nothing wrong. You like that muffin?"

She chuckled. "Yes. I love strawberries so these are my favorite muffins." As they ate, Brianna couldn't stand not knowing any longer. "Have you decided whether you're going to keep the ranch or sell it?"

He didn't say anything for a moment. "I've decided to keep the ranch."

A huge smile spread across her face and she couldn't contain her happiness. "You have?"

"Yes. However, there's something I need to talk to you about."

"Oh? What?" she asked, wondering what that could be.

"I want to get the most use out of the ranch and think I can by turning it back into a dude ranch, as well as making it into a thriving horse ranch. There's certainly enough land for both. However, there is a slight problem," he said.

"What's the problem, Cash?"

"Although there are plenty of water holes on the property, they tend to dry up. Before making a final decision, I have to be sure a permanent stream of water will be available for the horses. The best roaming and grazing areas for them are on land near Keystone River. However, only a small portion of the lake is on the section of Blazing Frontier that I own. The largest part of the lake is on the land Ellen gave to you."

He paused and then said, "I need to buy that section of land from you, Brianna."

Cash watched her take another sip of her coffee. She hadn't said anything, although he was certain she had heard him. If she needed time to digest what he'd said, he would give it to her.

A few seconds ticked by before she finally spoke. "I have no problem leasing fifty acres to you, Cash."

"But I'd have a problem with it."

"Why?" she asked.

"Because such an agreement isn't permanent. The amount of money that my investors and business partners will put into this ranch to bring it up to par can't hinge on such an agreement. What happens when the lease expires?"

"Then we enter into a new one," she said.

"We would negotiate for a new one with the hopes that both you and I are happy with the terms. What if we aren't? That would place my investors and business partners at risk."

She studied the contents of her coffee cup before glancing back at him. "Your offer is unexpected. I need time to think about it."

Cash released a sigh. "I wish I could say take all the time you need, but I can't. I will need to know by Friday, Brianna. I'd like to start work on this place before the end of the month."

"That soon?"

He smiled. "Yes, that soon," he said, starting to feel excited about it. "A number of repairs are needed, including a new roof on this house, the barn and several of the cottages. We also need to upgrade the game center and renovate the pool area."

Brianna nodded. "I will have my answer to you by Friday, Cash."

"Thank you. If there was any way I could do what's needed without the fifty acres, I would, but I can't. Otherwise, I will have to sell the ranch to someone who won't need as much water as I will."

"I understand."

Cash wondered if she honestly did. If he put the ranch up for sale, he would have to consider all offers. He was a businessman, after all. But then, what she'd shared with him about Sutherland bothered him deeply, and he knew it bothered her. Therefore, he would not be entertaining an offer from Sutherland, no matter what.

They finished their coffee and muffins in silence. Then he asked, "Where do we start with going through Ellen's belongings."

Brianna pushed her empty plate and coffee cup aside. "Last week I finished in her bedroom after you called to say you were coming. I donated her clothes and shoes to charity." She chuckled softly. "Ms. Ellen had over a zillion pairs."

"She liked shoes, huh?" Cash said.

"Yes."

"So do I. My brothers claim I own more shoes than I will ever wear."

"Then that's something you and Ms. Ellen had in common."

Cash said nothing to that comment as he got up from the table. "So, what's the plan for today?"

She glanced up at him. "We can do the attic."

A few minutes later, Cash followed Brianna and tried not to notice the sexy shape of her backside when she walked ahead of him up the stairs, but he couldn't help doing so. And she smelled good, too. Trying to take his mind off the sexy woman in front of him, he made a mental note to install sturdier railings for the stairs.

When she opened the attic door, he had expected to find a cluttered area but saw the place was tidy, filled with several filing cabinets. Instead of boxes, there were stacks of bins lined in neat rows against the walls.

Cash followed her into the room and saw how spacious the attic was. It didn't have a window, or central air and heat. The room could be converted into a nice-size office. It was on the far end of the hall and in a private corner.

Brianna glanced over at him. "While in high school, I used to earn my money each summer by keeping the attic neat."

He nodded. "What's in the bins?"

"Most contain ranch records dating back to heaven knows when."

"Any reason this stuff can't be shredded?" he asked her.

"No, but the only shredder we have is located behind the check-in desk downstairs," she told him.

"I'll haul it up here, no problem." He rolled up his sleeves. "Okay, let's get started."

They worked in companionable silence for the next couple hours. He had turned on the one ceiling fan in the room, but the air still wasn't circulating sufficiently. He noticed Brianna had rolled up the sleeves of her blouse.

After wiping sweat off his brow a few times, he said, "It's hot as the dickens in here. Mind if I take off my shirt?"

She looked over at him. "No, I don't mind."

"Thanks."

He began taking off his shirt, knowing her gaze was on him. He tried not to make it obvious that he knew she was watching him even though she was pretending she wasn't.

He inwardly smiled.

Brianna would not have minded if Cash had removed his pants as well.

From the first, she had thought he had a nice physique. He looked good in whatever he wore, whether it was a business suit or Western wear. She was just as convinced that he would look good wearing nothing at all.

She didn't want to stare and tried not to make it so obvious she was looking, but she knew he was unbuttoning his shirt and was aware of the exact moment he removed it to show a T-shirt. When he pulled the T-shirt over his head, her pulse began racing.

His muscular bare chest and strong biceps were the kind any woman would want to glide her hands across. Or better yet, she would love to bury her face in the curly hair covering his chest while inhaling his masculine scent. The visual that flowed through her mind nearly made her weak in the knees. Sweaty and sexy was one hell of a powerful combination for any woman to handle. Especially a woman whose hormones were acting out of whack.

"Brianna?"

Her gaze jerked up to his face, and when she saw the smile that curved his lips, she knew she'd been caught staring. "Yes?" she answered in a voice too husky to be her own.

"I just want you to know if it gets too hot in here for you, you can take your shirt off, too."

Cash's gaze lowered to her chest and her nipples hardened. "No, thanks," she said and quickly turned back to finish going through all the papers in one of the bins.

They continued to work in silence and when she glanced over at him again, she saw the rippling muscles of his back when he leaned down to pick up a bin to move it to another area. She forced down a moan and quickly looked away.

He evidently heard it. "Are you okay, Brianna?"

He had a sensual way of saying her name. It seemed to flow from his lips like warm honey. "Yes, I'm fine."

It was getting too hot in here for her and she knew if she didn't get out of this room with Cash, she wouldn't be liable for her actions. Glancing at her watch, she saw they had worked until a little past noon.

"How about if I make lunch?"

He turned and wiped sweat from his brow. "That sounds good. Dano left the fridge stocked, but I'm not sure with what."

"No problem. I'll check to see what I can whip up."

Brianna moved to rush by him, but the heel of her shoe caught on something and she went tumbling.

Right into Cash's arms.

Eleven

Cash caught Brianna, but he was not ready to release her yet. When she'd tripped, her face had landed on his chest, and she still had it there. He figured she needed a moment to get her bearings. That was fine with him.

"Are you alright?" he finally asked her.

Brianna lifted her head, but didn't try to pull away. "Sorry, Cash. I'm not usually clumsy."

There was something sexy about the movement of her throat while she talked. That, combined with such a luscious mouth, sent an adrenaline rush all through him. "No problem. I'm more than happy to catch you anytime."

"Thank you. I'm fine and you can release me now."

Could he? Did he want to? Brianna was the only woman alive who had the ability to shoot his libido up just from the sound of her too-sexy voice. "What if I said I prefer not to?"

She lifted an arched brow as she tipped her head back to look up at him. "Why not?"

"Because of this." Tightening his hold on her elbows, he eased her closer while leaning down to capture her mouth. He paused, waiting for her response, and was rewarded with her leaning in, too.

There was just something gratifying about kissing Brianna. Mating his mouth with hers was intense and so damn pleasurable. There was nothing like sliding his tongue into her mouth and then sucking on her tongue. He liked devouring her mouth in a way that made the muscles in his stomach quiver and the lower part of his body throb.

The deeper he took the kiss, the greedier he became. From the way she was moaning, he knew that she felt it, too. How would it be if they ever made love? They would burn up the sheets and be as sexually compatible as any couple could get.

She suddenly pulled her mouth away and rested her forehead against his chest as they tried to get their breathing under control. She finally lifted her head and looked at him in a way that tightened his gut. He saw her wet lips and glassy eyes, which made his libido soar even more.

"Why do you always kiss me?"

Did she honestly have to ask him that? "I believe your mouth is made for kissing. I can't think of any other woman I'd rather kiss, Brianna."

"I'm not very good at it."

He didn't think she was fishing for a compliment,

which meant she honestly thought that. He had no problem putting that assumption to rest. "You *are* good at it, Brianna. You're a natural. That's what makes kissing you so refreshing as well as enjoyable."

She took a step back and dropped her arms from him, "I need to go make lunch now."

"Okay."

She headed for the door, paused a moment and then looked back at him. "I think kissing you is refreshing and enjoyable, too, Cash."

Brianna's heart was pounding hard in her chest. Being around Cash did that to her. Then, whenever he would kiss her, she not only had to deal with her increased heart rate but also lost all sense. Telling Cash that she enjoyed his kisses, too, probably hadn't been a smart thing to do.

Walking over to the refrigerator, she opened it and pulled out everything she needed to make sandwiches, grateful Dano had purchased enough. She had finished making the turkey, ham and cheese sandwiches, to be served with a pitcher of iced tea, when she heard Cash behind her. Turning around, she saw he had at least put his T-shirt back on.

With great effort she tried maintaining her composure. "Just in time for lunch. I have it ready."

"Okay."

Whether he said one word or several, his deeply male voice had a way of stroking her senses. "I'll go wash up," he said. "I'll be back."

She watched him leave. He had such a masculine

walk. His long legs and tight thighs clad in jeans were pure male perfection.

By the time he returned, she had placed their plates on the table. "Thanks for fixing lunch, Brianna. It looks good."

"You are welcome. I think we accomplished a lot so far."

Cash glanced over at her and smiled. "Yes, we have. But we still have a lot more to do. I had no idea there was so much stuff." He paused a moment. "Now I feel bad about expecting you to do it on your own. That was selfish of me."

"No, it wasn't," she said, although she had thought that very thing at the time. "You had no idea all that stuff was up there."

He nodded. "I thought it would just be Ellen's personal things that you'd be more equipped to handle than I would."

For several seconds they said nothing while they ate. Then, out of the clear blue sky, he broke the silence. "You know what?"

She glanced over at him. "No, what?"

"Kissing you brings out the lust in me."

"Oh." She honestly didn't know what to say to that.

"Is there a part of me that brings out the lust in you, Brianna?"

Just because he'd asked didn't mean she had to answer. "I'd rather not say."

In truth, every part of him brought out the lust in her. The way his clothes fit. His smile. That dimple in his right cheek. The touch of his hands. His scent.

The magnetism of his eyes could draw her in whenever she gazed directly into them. She could go on and on.

"What if I want you to say?" he asked her.

Those eyes were drawing her in now. She broke contact to look down at her plate. When she glanced back across the table at him, she said, "We can't always have what we want, Cash."

Brianna's words were still weighing heavily on Cash's mind when they returned to the attic. Just like that morning, they worked in companionable silence. The only time they exchanged words was when she asked him about a particular document he'd come across.

He had hauled the shredder up two flights of stairs, and the humming sound helped as she fed documents into it. It didn't help whenever he looked over at her and caught her staring at him, or those times she had caught him staring at her.

He glanced at his watch when he felt a stirring of sexual desire again. "I think we should call it a day."

She looked over at him. "You won't get any complaints out of me. I think we got a lot accomplished."

Cash thought so, too. He watched her pull down the sleeves of her blouse, and then, to make it not so obvious that he was staring, he grabbed his shirt and put it back on. "What are your plans for this evening?" he asked her.

She looked up at him. "I don't have any. Why?"

"I'd like you to spend it with me."

She pushed her hair from her face. "Spend it with you how?"

He could tell her a lot of naughty ways, but instead he said, "I'd like to see what the town has to offer in the way of fun."

She didn't say anything for a moment. "It just so happens the state fair came to town this weekend, if you're looking for something fun to do."

He smiled over at her. "Then let's do it."

They did do it.

Brianna had to admit she had fun. It wasn't just that Cash had taken her to grab something to eat at the town's favorite pizzeria, or that he'd won a huge stuffed bear for her, or that he'd shared his foot-long hot dog with her. It had been how he had walked around holding her hand and hadn't seemed bothered that doing so caught the attention of a number of people.

The one thing that had surprised her was that when they had reached her house, he'd declined her invitation for coffee. But he'd made up for it in the kiss that still had her swooning an hour or so later.

She had just showered and gotten into bed when her phone rang. She recognized the number and her heart began pounding. "Yes?"

"Go to sleep and think about me tonight."

She was tempted to tell Cash that she would do more than just think about him. Deciding to be coy, she smiled and said, "Now, why should I do that?"

"Because you like me."

Yes, she most certainly did. "Maybe."

"Where is Magnum?"

Cash had named the huge stuffed bear Magnum. "He's right here in bed with me."

"I envy that bear."

She didn't say anything but swore she could feel the crackle of sexual energy through the phone. "What are you doing? In bed yet?"

"Nope. I'm sitting outside on the porch enjoying a beer. What time can I expect you tomorrow?"

"Around nine. I forgot to mention I have an appointment on Thursday so I won't be coming that day." No way would she tell him what the appointment was about.

"Okay, I will see you tomorrow. Give Magnum a pat on his head for me."

She chuckled. "I will. Good night."

"Good night, Brianna."

She had just finished giving Magnum his pat on the head when Brianna's cell phone rang again. She smiled, recognizing the ringtone, and quickly answered it. "Miesha?"

"Yes. I had to put Darrett to bed and then prepare for a meeting with my employees in the morning. But I wanted to know how things went this weekend. Was Cashen Outlaw as hot as ever?"

Brianna chuckled. "Yes." She then told her friend about the weekend.

"When will he make a decision as to whether or not he'll keep the ranch or sell it?"

"Cash already has. He plans to keep it."

After Miesha released a huge yell, Brianna added, "However, there might be a glitch."

"What kind of glitch?"

Brianna nibbled on her bottom lip. "His decision is dependent on me," she said.

"How so?"

Brianna then told Miesha what Cash had told her about the fifty acres.

"He wants your land?" And before Brianna could answer, Miesha exclaimed, "Wow! Now you have bargaining power."

Bargaining power? Brianna lifted a brow. "What on earth are you talking about?"

"Think about it, Brie. You have something he wants, and he has something you want."

Brianna shook her head. "And just what is it he has that I want?"

"Sperm. And I bet he has plenty of them."

Brianna blinked. "What!"

"Why bother going to that fertility clinic on Thursday? Cashen Outlaw would be the logical person to father your child."

"How on earth do you figure that?"

"Because more than once you mentioned he was handsome, but you also said he was intelligent and kind. Those would be great traits to pass on to your child. If you recall, it was just last week when I suggested you place him at the top of the list."

"Yes, I recall the conversation, but at the time you were joking," Brianna said.

"At the time, you didn't have bargaining power. Now you do. I bet the two of you could work out a doozy of a deal if he wants your fifty acres bad enough."

"I don't know, Miesha," Brianna said, not convinced doing something like that was a good idea.

"Think about it, Brianna. You'd know the identity of

your baby's father. And more importantly, your baby would know the identity of his father. If Cash Outlaw doesn't like the idea, he can tell you no."

"He *will* tell me no."

"You'll never know if you don't ask."

A short while later, Brianna settled in her favorite position in bed while thinking about Miesha's suggestion. There was no way Cash would go along with such a thing. *Would he?*

But what if he would for the fifty acres?

If he went along with it, and agreed with her terms, at least her child would have a vested interest in both her land and Cash's. But would he see it that way?

Deciding she didn't want to think about it anymore tonight, she did just what Cash had asked her to do earlier. She went to sleep and thought about him.

Twelve

Cash glanced at his watch, expecting Brianna to arrive any minute. It was hard to believe it was the end of the week. She had arrived at the ranch at nine and they would work together until around four in the afternoon. Usually they would break for lunch at noon.

Since she had prepared lunch for them on Monday, he had treated her on Tuesday to Monroe's. On Wednesday, she had brought lunch from home. Cash enjoyed sharing meals with her and liked getting to know her better.

It had become a habit for him to greet her each morning with a brush across the lips. He also gave her the same kind of kiss when he walked her to the door each evening. Cash was trying to practice restraint where Brianna was concerned, not wanting to overwhelm her or sway her decision about the fifty acres in any way. He saw that as business and what was between them as personal.

Yesterday Brianna had taken the day off for an appointment she had in Jackson, Wyoming. He had missed her. Although they would go hours while working through the stuff in the attic without holding a conversation, he would still feel her presence. More than once yesterday he'd glanced over to where she would normally be working and felt lonely knowing she wasn't there.

How would he handle things at the end of next week when he left to return to Fairbanks? He didn't want to think about that. It took a lot for a woman to capture his interest—and what felt like his very existence.

Maybe that's why he was standing on the porch waiting for Brianna to arrive this morning. He knew the moment her car pulled into the driveway. He stood, leaning against one of the posts, and watched her get out of the car. She looked pretty today, wearing a long, flowing printed skirt and pink blouse.

In truth, he thought she looked pretty every day. The moment she set foot on the porch, he walked over to her, pulled her into his arms and kissed her. In broad daylight. Not caring if the foreman or any of the ranch hands saw them. And it wasn't a mere brush across the lips.

He needed to taste her, mingle his tongue with hers, hold her close in his arms and inhale her scent. When he finally released her, he could tell by the look on her face that she had been surprised by his bold action. His public display of affection.

"Welcome back, Brianna," he said, but not before

giving her lips another swipe with his tongue. "You look beautiful this morning. I love seeing you in the color pink."

She smiled up at him with moist lips. "Do you?"

"Yes, most definitely. It brings out the beauty of your eyes even more."

"Um, flattery will get you everywhere. Should I assume you missed me yesterday, Cash?"

He chuckled. "Yes, you can assume that. I went into town earlier and grabbed take-out breakfast from Brewster's Café. All we have to do is warm it up."

"Thanks. Did you get a lot done yesterday while I was gone?" she asked, following him into the house.

"No," he said, deciding to be honest. "I was bored."

"Poor baby."

He chuckled. "Yes, poor baby."

Cash warmed up the food in the microwave, and whenever he glanced over at her, she was staring out the kitchen window as if deep in thought. It was Friday. Did she remember that today she was to give him an answer on the fifty acres?

What if she didn't want to sell the land to him? He honestly didn't want to think about that possibility, although the businessman in him thought he should. He would admit being here on the ranch for the past nine days had spoiled him. Or could it be that he hadn't realized how much he had needed a break from Outlaw Freight Lines, and that any place would have worked?

He refused to believe that. He had a feeling it had everything to do with waking up at daybreak and breathing in the brisk Wyoming air.

And maybe spending time with Brianna.

He set the plates in front of her and then poured the coffee into cups before joining her at the table. The pensive look on her face bothered him. "Brianna, is anything wrong?"

Brianna shook her head. "No, why do you ask?"

"Usually you're more talkative than you are this morning."

Yes, usually she was. There was no way she would tell him that her meeting in Jackson at the fertility clinic hadn't gone quite the way she'd hoped. Everyone at the facility had been nice and positive, yet when she reviewed the bios of the men they'd selected for her to consider, she had found them all lacking.

Now she wished Miesha hadn't planted that seed in her head about Cash becoming the father of her child.

"I just have a lot on my mind."

"Anything I can help you with?"

If only you knew, she thought. Instead she said, "It's something I need to deal with on my own."

"Alright. If you change your mind, let me know."

She nodded. She would be letting him know soon enough. They didn't say much as they climbed the stairs to the attic, and once there moved to their respective areas of the room.

As she was about to go through the bins, she found an envelope with her name on it. She glanced over at Cash, but he had his back to her. She opened the envelope to find a note.

I really did miss you yesterday.
Cash

Brianna couldn't help but smile as a warm feeling flowed through her. It touched her deeply that he'd missed her and hadn't had a problem letting her know it.

She thought he deserved the same. "Cash?"

He turned around. "Yes?"

She gave him a bright smile. "I missed you yesterday, too."

He returned her smile. "Good."

Was it good? Would he still think it was good after she told him the decision she had made about the fifty acres? A decision that had taken her a few sleepless nights and thought-provoking days to ponder.

It hadn't been easy, but Miesha was right. Brianna couldn't think of any other man she would want to father her child. There were a number of reasons she felt that way, but she knew the main one—the one she could not deny—was that she had fallen in love with Cash.

Brianna honestly believed a part of her had given him her heart that day, close to nine years ago, when she had come across his picture. Whether he knew it or not, he had replaced the pain in her heart with hope. Seemed that was still true.

"I guess we better get to work," she then said, rolling up her sleeves.

Pretty soon a few hours had passed and Cash said it was time to stop for lunch. Glancing over at him, she said, "I'm not hungry. I think I'll work through lunch."

He stared at her for a minute and then nodded. "I'm not hungry either. I suggest we work for couple more hours and then call it a day."

It seemed as if the two hours had rushed by when

he said, "That's it for today. How about if we share a glass of lemonade?"

"Sounds good," she said, moving across the room.

She was walking past him when he reached out and took her hand, studying her features. "Are you sure you're okay, Brianna?"

She was about to nod and tell him yes, and then thought better of it. It was time for her to give him her answer about the land and then face the consequences.

"I need to tell you my decision about the land, Cash."

He leaned against a wall, still holding her hand. "And what is your decision?"

She nervously nibbled on her bottom lip as she looked at him. "I will sign over all fifty acres to you, Cash, free and clear, if you give me something in return."

He bunched his forehead. The look on his face clearly showed his bemusement. "And what is that?"

Brianna didn't say anything as she nervously gnawed on her bottom lip and glanced away. She needed to focus on anything but him. She could feel the heat of his stare on every part of her body.

After forcing a deep whoosh of air through her lungs, she said, "I will *give* you the fifty acres, Cash, in exchange for your sperm."

Thirteen

Cash stared at Brianna. There was no way she'd said what he thought she'd said. He must have misunderstood. "Excuse me, but could you repeat that?"

She held his gaze and repeated it.

So she *had* said that. "My sperm?"

"Yes."

"Why do you need my sperm?"

"Because I want a baby."

Duh, Cash thought. That had been a stupid question for him to ask. What other reason would there be for a woman to need a man's sperm? "Why do you want a baby? You aren't married."

"If I was married, I wouldn't be needing your sperm. You don't have to be married to have a baby, Cash."

He knew that. Maybe he wasn't asking the right

questions. Maybe it was the heat in the attic frying his brain cells, or the fact that normally, women didn't go around asking men for their sperm. "Let's get out of here." He needed something to drink, and for him it had to be something stronger than lemonade. "We're going to sit down at my kitchen table and you're going to tell me what the hell is going on, Brianna."

"That's fine."

"After you," he said, standing back for her to move ahead of him. He hung back a minute to get himself together.

When they reached the kitchen, she went straight to the refrigerator for the lemonade and he went to the liquor cabinet. He pulled down a bottle of vodka and a shot glass.

When he walked back to the table, she was already seated, staring into her glass. She looked nervous. Hopefully, that meant she didn't make it a habit of going around asking a man for his sperm. He honestly didn't think she did, but he would know for certain in a minute.

He slid into the chair across from her, placed both the bottle of vodka and the shot glass on the table and poured. "So, why a baby and why *my* sperm, Brianna?"

Brianna took a sip of lemonade before she said, "I've always wanted a family, Cash. I was an only child, so I dreamed of one day getting married, becoming a mom with lots of kids. At least four. Alan had wanted a large family, too. That was one of the things we agreed on."

She paused. "I had everything planned. We would marry like he promised, the year I graduated from high school, and I would travel with him and support his military career and have his babies. It was my dream to have all four before my thirtieth birthday."

She couldn't help but smile at the lifting of his brow. "I know that sounds crazy because it means my being pregnant most of the time, but I was okay with that. Alan was, too. The kids would each be two years apart. Like I said, I had it all planned out."

The smile on Brianna's face faded when she continued. "But none of those plans happened. My dreams were destroyed."

He nodded. "Yes, you told me."

She took another sip of her lemonade. "Nobody knew how much I wanted a family more than my parents. Especially Dad. I think at one time that's all I ever talked about. Marrying Alan, being a good wife to him and a good mother to our babies. Dad knew the pain Alan's betrayal caused me and I told him I would never marry. He believed me."

Brianna paused again. "Dad knew he was dying and wanted to prepare me for a life without him. He didn't want me to be alone. He knew it was likely I would never fall in love and marry, which meant I would never have a child and be the mother I'd always wanted to be."

She fought back tears. "The night before he died, Dad sat me down on the sofa beside him and made me promise him that I wouldn't be alone on my thirtieth birthday. And that I would have the one thing I'd always wanted."

"A baby?"

"Yes."

He looked at her. "A child and not a husband?"

"Yes. Dad figured I would get pregnant without a man's involvement like Miesha did."

He lifted a brow. "Who's Miesha?"

"Miesha James is my best friend from college. She still lives in Atlanta and owns a communications firm there. For reasons I'd rather not go into, Miesha wanted a baby, so she went to a sperm bank. She had the procedure done, got pregnant, and now Darrett is six and in first grade." Brianna paused. "Dad figured right. I had planned to do the same thing when it came time to have my baby."

She took another sip of her lemonade. "However, I recently discovered the sperm bank might not be the best approach to motherhood after all."

"Why not?"

She poured more lemonade before answering. "It was a hard decision to make, but there were no donors there who felt right to me."

"Why me, Brianna? Why would you want me to father your child?"

Brianna gave him the reasons that had convinced her she would be doing the right thing. "You are kind, thoughtful and caring, Cash. Besides, you don't live here. You said you would be living in Alaska and would hire someone to run the ranch for you. That means I could raise the child on my own. You and I wouldn't have to see each other. But more than anything, I believe you would do right by our child and take responsibility for him or her if something happened to me."

When he didn't say anything, she pressed on. "I wouldn't want anything from you, Cash. This won't be a love match and I'll sign any papers waiving my rights to your possessions. I can afford to raise my child on my own. This will strictly be a business arrangement. You get the fifty acres. All I want is your sperm."

"How?"

Now she was the one lifting a brow. "How what?"

"How am I supposed to give you this sperm, Brianna?"

By asking that question, did that mean he was at least considering it? "By artificial insemination. That way you won't have to be concerned about any physical contact between us."

Brianna stood, took her glass over to the sink and washed it out, noting he hadn't said anything. She came back to stand by the table. "I realize you're going to need time to think about it, Cash. However, if you can let me know something by next week, I would appreciate it."

Without saying anything else, she grabbed her purse off the counter and walked out the door.

Cash sat at the kitchen table until he heard Brianna's car drive off. Then he threw back the shot of vodka.

He wanted fifty acres of Brianna's land and she wanted to use his sperm to have a baby. By artificial insemination.

A slow heat stirred in his groin when he thought of another way that he could share his sperm with her. He quickly brushed the thought from his mind because he wasn't sharing his sperm with anybody. What made her think that if he got a woman pregnant, he wouldn't want to be a part of the child's life?

Damn that guy who had destroyed all her dreams of becoming a mother and wife. Now she was willing to become a mother without a husband. She deserved her whole dream. She said she thought Cash was kind and caring. Well, he thought the same thing about her. He had seen firsthand how she'd gotten along with his cousins and friends last weekend. And those times when he had accompanied her in town, it was obvious to him how well liked she was.

The one thing she was wrong about was her assumption that she knew Cash. If she did, then she would know there was no way he would get a woman pregnant and not want to be a part of his child's life. Especially after his mother had chosen not to be a part of his. He would not make that same mistake with his own child.

Then there was the way she said she would get pregnant. Artificial insemination? Not hardly. And what did she say about eliminating any concern about physical contact between them? Did she honestly think that was a concern of his? Especially when there had been an overabundance of sexual chemistry between them from the start?

Brianna never did say what would happen if he didn't go along with this idea of hers. Did that mean she would approach someone else? He rubbed his hands down his face in frustration. The bottom line was that there was something he wanted more than those fifty acres of land.

He wanted her.

She wanted them to handle this like a business deal. In that case, she would see just how he operated. Other than Garth, Cash was the Outlaw who didn't pull any punches when it came to negotiation. When he had a challenge, he overcame it each and every time. He could be steadfast and unmovable, and could play hard better than anyone. In other words, when confronted with opposition, he could be a force to reckon with.

Cash grabbed his Stetson off the hat rack as he headed for the door. He intended to ride around the range and was confident that when he returned, he would have come up with a plan.

Brianna had eaten and cleaned up the kitchen by the time the sun went down. She had then showered and changed into a comfortable sundress. Now she was enjoying a glass of wine in the swing on the porch.

She couldn't help wondering if Cash was giving her proposition any thought. Asking a man to father her child was a very bold thing to do. But then, desperation would give a person the courage to do just about anything. She had given him until next week for an answer, but what if he didn't agree to it? Would she withhold the land from him? Probably not, but at least she would have tried playing her hand.

Hearing the sound of a car approaching, she tilted her head to see the driveway. It was Cash. Her heart began beating fast in her chest, like it did whenever Cash was around.

Why was he coming here? Did that mean he had made a decision already? If he had, that also meant he really hadn't given her proposal much thought. Was he here to tell her he had no intention of being the father of her baby?

Placing her wineglass aside, she stood when he came up the steps. She saw he had that just-showered look and had changed into another pair of jeans and a Western shirt. He smelled good. Too good.

Whatever he'd come here to say, the best thing would be for him to say it and leave.

"Hello, Brianna."

The deep, throaty sound of his voice put sensuous goose bumps on her arms. "Cash? I am surprised to see you. Is anything wrong?"

"No. I came to deliver my answer to your proposition."

It was just as she'd assumed. He hadn't given it much thought if he was turning her down already. "I was enjoying a glass of wine. Would you like one?"

"I prefer a beer if you have one."

"I do. Come on in," she said, entering the house.

He followed her into the kitchen and leaned against one of the counters. "You've eaten already?"

She grabbed the beer out of the refrigerator. "Yes. If you want something, I—"

"No, thanks," he interrupted to say. "I have a taste for a hamburger and fries and was on my way to Monroe's."

She nodded, handing him the beer. "You're getting addicted to the place like the rest of us."

"Looks that way." He took a slug of his beer and then licked his lips.

Watching him do that made her pulse rate increase. She didn't want to wring her hands together but was doing so anyway. "What is your answer?"

"I'm here to make you a counteroffer, Brianna."

That's not what she'd expected to hear. "A counteroffer?"

"Yes."

"What kind of counteroffer?"

Covering the distance separating them, he came to stand in front of her. She tilted her head back to look up at him. "I will give you the baby you want, but there will be something I want from you," he said.

Brianna lifted an arched brow. "In addition to the fifty acres?"

"Yes, in addition to the fifty acres."

She nervously licked her lips, not knowing what that could be. "What is it you want from me?"

"Marriage."

Fourteen

Cash saw Brianna's eyes widen. "Marriage?"

"Yes, marriage. The only way you can have my sperm is to marry me. Also, when I get you pregnant, it won't be by any insemination procedure. It will be the traditional way with us sharing a bed as husband and wife."

He saw the color drain from Brianna's face.

"But why would you want us to get married? That doesn't make sense," she said, honestly looking confused.

"I happen to think it makes perfect sense. You want my baby and I want marriage."

She shook her head as if still not understanding. "But why would you want marriage?"

"There are a number of reasons. The foremost is that I'll be thirty-five at the end of the year and it's time for me to settle down," he said, knowing it was a bald-faced lie even as the words flowed from his lips. He could have gone through life and never married, and he certainly hadn't given any thought to settling down before now. But she didn't have to know that.

"What do you mean, 'it's time'?"

He shrugged. "What I mean is that it is expected. My older brother Garth married last year. My brother Jess would be next in line to tie the knot, but he'll need a wife who wants to be married to a politician, so we're giving him more time."

He took another swig of his beer. "Being married comes in handy when you're negotiating business deals with men with single daughters who think it should be a package deal."

Brianna frowned. "But I have no intention of ever moving to Alaska."

"And I have no intention of ever living here. For us, it wouldn't matter since our marriage will only be a business deal." That was another lie. "I will come and visit from time to time to see my child."

She didn't say anything for a minute and then asked, "In other words, you want the status and not a real marriage?"

A smile touched his lips. "No, I wouldn't say that. I want all the things that come with being married, including sharing my wife's bed."

Before she could respond, he said, "I think there is something you should know about me, Brianna. Because of the kind of relationship I had with Ellen, there is no way I would want to have that same kind of relationship with a child I created. There is no way on this earth I could get you pregnant and then pretend you and the child didn't exist."

"What about other women?" she asked.

He lifted a brow. "Other women?"

"Yes. Although it wouldn't be a traditional marriage, would you still stick to your marriage vows or would you feel you have the right to sleep with other women?"

He held her gaze, needing to make sure she understood him. "You will be the only woman I make love to, Brianna. And I expect the same on your end."

When she didn't say anything, he pressed on, hoping what he was about to offer would be the icing on the cake.

"Also, as my wife, you will share the Blazing Frontier with me. All of it, and not just what Ellen left to you. If anything were to happen to me while we are married, it will belong to you and our child."

She stared at him. "Since you are demanding marriage, how long will this marriage have to last?"

Demand? Was he demanding marriage? Yes, in a way he was. "Forever."

"Forever!"

He crossed his arms over his chest. "Yes, forever."

"Impossible. I told you I never intend to marry."

"And I refuse to get a woman pregnant without marriage. Then, after that, it is important that I remain married to the woman for my child's sake. I refuse to divorce my child's mother the way my father did his wives."

She didn't say anything for a moment, then asked, "Just what will this marriage entail?"

He dropped his hands to his sides. "I've told you one aspect of it, regarding our sleeping arrangements. I also mentioned you didn't have to move to Alaska unless at some point you wanted to. Most of my time will be in Alaska, but I will visit here from time to time to see my child."

"And the ranch?"

"As part owner, you can run the dude ranch like before. The horse training and breeding part of it will require help and you will get it."

"You're entrusting me with all the Blazing Frontier's business?" she asked in amazement.

"As my wife and business partner, I see no reason I shouldn't. However, there is the matter of the times you might need off during your pregnancies."

"Pregnancies?"

He smiled. "Yes, pregnancies. Like you, I also want a lot of children and agree that four sounds good." That wasn't true since he honestly hadn't ever thought of having children until she'd made her request. But if she wanted four babies, he could certainly give them to her.

"Who knows? Multiple births run in my family, so we might hit the jackpot and have triplets or twins, which will decrease the number of times you'd be pregnant." He only added that part because he'd overheard her tell his cousin Bane that she would love to have twins or triplets.

"What do you think of my counteroffer, Brianna?"

She was nibbling on her lips and wringing her hands together. "I need time to think about it."

"Okay. I want your answer on Monday morning."

She drew in a deep breath. "If I decide to go along with your counteroffer, Cash, how soon would you want this marriage to take place?"

"Within forty-eight hours of when you say yes."

Her eyes widened. "Why the rush?"

He raised a brow. "Maybe I misunderstood you earlier today, but didn't you say something about wanting a child before your thirtieth birthday? I figured you would want to get started on one right away. I plan to leave for Alaska next weekend. After that, you will have to let me know your body's best time for fertilization, and then I'll make arrangements to return."

Cash knew he was giving her the impression that the only reason he would make love to her was for a baby. His goal was that making love would be so enjoyable that she would want to continue for more than just making a baby.

"Why not artificial insemination?"

He placed the empty beer bottle on the table, deciding not to answer. He glanced at his watch. "I need to leave to get something to eat. Will I have your decision Monday morning, Brianna?"

She released a deep breath and then said, "Yes, you'll have it."

He leaned down and brushed a kiss across her lips. "This way, we both get what we want, Brianna."

And then he turned and left.

"What are you going to do, Brie?"

Sitting on her back patio, Brianna looked over the land she was proud to call hers while sipping her coffee. It was her second cup that morning after getting up early, before sunrise, after a sleepless night thinking about Cash's counteroffer.

"I don't know, Miesha. None of what he is offering is what I asked for."

"Yes, but you're getting a whole lot more. Just think. He is offering marriage."

Brianna rolled her eyes. "He is *demanding* marriage, Miesha. Why can't he just do things my way?"

"I think he's told you why. Cash Outlaw wants a wife, not a woman to impregnate. He wants more than one child, just like you do, and he prefers the same woman birthing his children. I can appreciate that. What I appreciate even more is that he is willing to share what's his with you."

Hoping she had Brianna thinking, Miesha pressed on. "Just think. He is giving you control of the ranch. Not as an employee but as co-owner. That sounds pretty darn generous to me. Some men would stick you with a prenup so fast your head would spin. Don't let your hang-up about never getting married keep you from what I see as a pretty darn good deal."

Brianna took another sip of coffee. "It seems like he's trying to get the upper hand."

"Why? Because he's found a way to get you into his bed?"

"In a way, yes."

Miesha giggled. "Excuse me. But haven't you said his kisses left you so hot you were tempted to jump his bones?"

"I was all talk and you know it."

"Well, now you can put your 'all talk' into action. What are you afraid of?"

Brianna knew the answer to that question easily. Her heart.

"I got a crush on him from just looking at his picture, Miesha. What if I fall for him again? Harder this time. Do you know what that could do to me?"

"You were vulnerable back then because of Alan, and Cash Outlaw was your escape from reality. There was nothing wrong with that. If you recall, all the time I was pregnant, I fantasized Shemar Moore was my baby's daddy."

"I know, but—"

"But this is now, Brianna," Miesha interrupted to say. "If he's good to you and treats you right, would it be wrong to fall in love with him? He's not setting a time limit on your marriage. It sounds to me that he expects it to last. A lot of things can happen. A lot of emotions can develop on both sides."

"What about being the town's scandal again?" Brianna said.

"Honestly, girl? You were planning on having a baby without the benefit of a husband. How is marrying a man and having his baby more of a scandal than that? Think about it."

An hour later, Brianna had saddled Baby to go riding, and to think. Out on the open range, she couldn't help but laugh out loud as they raced across the plains and valleys. Because Baby was used to the land, Brianna allowed him the freedom to roam wherever he pleased. She was so caught up in her thoughts about

Cash's counteroffer that it took a while for Brianna to notice she was now on Blazing Frontier land.

She tightened her hold on Baby's reins to turn him back when she saw a lone rider galloping toward her.

Cash.

She quickly assessed her options. She could pretend she hadn't seen him and race Baby back home, or she could stay and acknowledge his presence. She chose the latter, but the closer he got, the more she wished she'd chosen the former.

It seemed every time she saw Cash, he was even more handsome than the last. He was sex-in-jeans, sex-drinking-a-beer and now sex-riding-a-horse. She'd thought the same thing the first time she saw him slide into a saddle, and watched how his thick, masculine thighs flanked the animal in a way that made Brianna want to fan herself.

He definitely knew how to handle a horse and sat erect in the saddle the way a rider was supposed to. He finally brought his horse to a stop a few feet from hers.

"Good morning, Cash."

"Good morning, Brianna." He tilted his Stetson in greeting. "Looks like we had the same idea. Nice morning for a ride," he said.

"Yes, it is."

"You're heading back?" he asked, looking at her intently.

"That was my plan," she said, holding tight to Baby's reins.

"Would you ride with me for a while?"

Brianna didn't think that was a good idea and should have declined his invitation. However, when those penetrating dark eyes stared at her, the next thing she knew, she was nodding her head.

They took off galloping across the plains, going deeper and deeper onto Blazing Frontier land. When they slowed the horses, she glanced over at him. He rode his horse well. Why on earth was she suddenly imagining him straddling her and then riding her the same way? The thought made a shiver rush through her, and when he watched her with such smoldering intensity, she suddenly felt extremely hot.

"I thought about you last night, Brianna."

She had news for him. She had thought about him, too. "Did you?"

"Yes. You might not know this, but lately you've taken my dreams hostage."

Probably no more than he had taken hers, but she was surprised he would admit such a thing. "Why?"

He chuckled, and the sound made even more intense heat pass through her. "That's easy enough to answer. I see you and I want you. I don't see you and I still want you. Point blank. I want you, Brianna."

Fifteen

"You shouldn't say such things, Cash."

He leaned back on his horse. "Why not? It's the truth. But you already know that, right? I'm sure my desire for you comes through loud and clear every time we kiss, and we've kissed quite a bit."

"Not this week."

She quickly looked away, as if she'd been embarrassed to make such an observation. Too late, she had made it. Did that mean she had missed their kisses as much as he had? That could easily be remedied, but first he felt the need to tell her why he had toned them down.

He brought his horse to a stop and so did she. "The reason I haven't kissed you much this week, Brianna, is that whenever I kiss you, I don't want to stop. I want to take it to the next level." He was certain she clearly understood what that next level was.

She looked back at him with a glare in her eyes, and he knew she'd taken offense. "Like I wouldn't have had anything to say about it?"

He smiled. "I'm sure you would have, but mostly what I would have heard from you would have been moans of pleasure."

While she angrily spluttered her denials, he dismounted. He then moved to her horse and reached up for her.

"What do you think you're doing?" she asked in a voice filled with annoyance as she batted his hands away.

"I am helping you down. The horses need to rest a spell. I won't bite you." But he sure as hell wouldn't mind kissing her.

She hesitated, but then, as if deciding he was right and the horses needed to rest, she took his hand. Then it happened. The moment their hands touched, total, complete and unharnessed awareness shot through his entire body. Cash glanced up at Brianna and knew without a doubt that she had felt it, too. There was no way she had not.

"Maybe I should go," she said in a soft voice.

"The horses need to rest, Brianna. You're safe here with me."

She gave him a doubtful look, but she didn't pull her hand away. When her feet touched the ground, she said, "Thanks, Cash." When he continued to hold her around her waist, she added, "You can let go of me now."

"Brianna…"

He was about to say something, but for the life of him, he wasn't sure what it was. So he tried again. "Brianna…"

She held his gaze and nervously licked her lips. "Yes?"

Instead of answering, he moved his hands to her waist and nudged her closer. Then, as if his mouth had a mind of its own, it lowered to hers.

The moment their mouths touched, Brianna felt her insides tingle as if she'd come in contact with a live wire. A series of responses, none she felt capable of controlling, ripped through her body. Cash's kisses were her weakness because she enjoyed them so much.

She knew she should push back, stop him from deepening the kiss more than he already had. But all her common sense left her, vibrated off into the wind. All she had the ability to do at that moment was get wrapped up in his incredible taste.

And it was incredible.

Brianna was convinced there was nothing else quite like it. Not that she had kissed a lot of guys, but Cash Outlaw's taste created a yearning within her that made her entire body ache.

He suddenly released her mouth, and she pulled in air and the scent of man through her nostrils. Then he was kissing her again, his mouth more demanding and greedier than before. She heard herself moan under the onslaught of the deep glides of his tongue.

Then she felt his hand leave her waist to fondle the buttons on her blouse. Brianna knew she should stop him, but that thought vanished when he deepened the kiss even further. She heard herself purr again as toe-curling sensations rippled through her.

She knew he had unbuttoned her shirt when she felt a breeze across her chest. He broke away from her mouth to trail tongue-licking kisses against her jaw and neck and along the edge of her collarbone.

"Cash…"

She closed her eyes, absorbing all the sensations he was making her feel. She hadn't realized he had used his fingers to undo the front clasp of her bra until his mouth was right there, sucking her nipple into his mouth.

Brianna threw her head back, and the movement seemed to thrust her nipple farther into him. He took advantage by exerting more pressure and sucking her nipple in earnest, like he'd been greedy for it forever.

Those actions made a series of moans flow from her lips at the same time she grasped the back of his head to hold his mouth right there. Never had she felt such intense desire.

She and Alan had made love only twice. The time right before he was supposed to leave for the military, and when he'd come home right before getting deployed to Germany. He had taken care of his own needs without hers, but at the time she hadn't minded.

Now she saw how selfish that was. He had never taken her breasts into his mouth and lapped on them the way Cash was doing. Suddenly, her entire body felt as if it was on fire.

Her body jerked. It seemed as if a bolt of light-ning had lanced through her and she convulsed in unthinkable pleasure. Brianna gasped aloud at the unexpected, unadulterated carnality that tore through her, then screamed Cash's name.

Then he was back at her mouth, kissing her while a barrage of sensations bombarded her, followed by spasms that ran through her body. He released her mouth and pulled her into his arms while gently stroking her back as the spasms continued.

"You're okay, sweetheart. I got you."

Brianna knew what had just happened. She had experienced her very first orgasm and it had been unbelievable. It had happened not in a bed but out on the plains. On Blazing Frontier land. If she had to do it again, she wouldn't change a thing. It had been natural and perfect.

"Brianna?"

She leaned forward and buried her face in Cash's chest, not ready for him to look at her yet. When he said her name again and asked if she was okay, she finally lifted her face and met his intense gaze. "Yes, I'm okay. And thank you."

He snapped her bra back in place and began rebuttoning her blouse. "What did you just thank me for?"

Brianna figured he had to know. A man with his experience could tell. He probably just wanted her to admit it. "I was thanking you for giving me pleasure. No man has ever done that before."

His hand on her buttons went still, and he glanced down at her. "Are you saying Alan never…"

"No. He never. We only made love twice and both times he was in a hurry."

Brianna saw the tight frown that settled over Cash's

face. "A real man is never in too much of a hurry to satisfy his woman."

She didn't know what to say to that. The only thing she knew was she needed to get away from him and fast before she was begging for an encore. When she took a step back, she nearly lost her balance from feeling weak in the knees. Totally drained.

"Hold still. I'm taking you home."

She lifted a brow. "How are you taking me home?"

"We're riding double on my horse. I'll tie Baby to the back."

"That's not necessary. Just put me on Baby. He knows the way home. I'm fine."

He just looked at her and said, "I'm taking you home, Brianna."

And as if that settled it, he lifted her up and placed her on his horse like she weighed nothing, before straddling his horse and holding her in front of him.

"You can lean back against me if you want," he invited.

She did. His chest felt strong, warm, comforting. Brianna closed her eyes, lulled by the slow rocking motion of the horse and the feel of resting her back against Cash's chest. She must have fallen asleep because she recalled him gently rubbing the side of her face to let her know they had arrived at her house.

He dismounted and then reached up for her. But he never let her feet touch the ground—he swept her from the horse into his arms.

"Cash, you can put me down."

He smiled down at her. "I will, but not now."

When they reached her door, he asked for her key.

She shifted in his arms to tug it out of her pocket and handed it to him. He opened the door and carried her inside and straight to her bedroom, where he placed her gently on the bed. Right next to Magnum. Then he backed up.

"I suggest you take a nap."

"A nap?"

"Yes."

She shook her head. "I'll take a nap later. I need to take care of Baby."

"I'll take care of Baby. You rest."

She frowned, tempted to tell him she'd had her first orgasm, not open heart surgery. "I'm fine, Cash. But I am curious about something."

"What?"

She began nibbling on her bottom lip, and she could tell he knew she was nervous about whatever it was she wanted to ask him. "You can ask me anything, Brianna."

"Are all of them like this? This powerful?"

His expression said he knew exactly what she was asking. "Most are way more powerful than that. On a scale of one to five with five as the max, you experienced a level-one."

Her eyes widened. "That's enough about levels of passion. Take a nap and rest. I'll stop by later to check on you."

She pulled to sit up and he gave her a look that had her easing back down. "You don't have to do that."

"I take care of what's mine, Brianna."

She glared at him. "I'm not yours."

"Not yet."

He moved toward the door, paused and glanced back at her. A smile curved his lips when he said, "If you want to experience a higher level of passion than you did today, Brianna, you'll have to marry me."

Brianna continued to lie in bed long after Cash left. Why was he so insistent that she marry him? And she wasn't sure she liked him assuming she was his. At that moment she couldn't help but remember their kiss and how it had moved to another level when he had put his mouth on her breasts.

Even now, her pulse kicked up thinking about it, and she could recall every single sensation that had swamped her body. She had been filled with pleasure she hadn't known anyone was capable of feeling.

What was happening to her? There was no doubt in her mind that Cash presented a temptation causing an edginess within her that couldn't be normal. At least not for her. And what had he said before leaving? She would not experience a higher level of passion with him until they got married.

She was convinced a higher level just might take her out. The thought of it made lust hum through her veins, had her pulse kicking, her nerves dancing and her brain becoming dysfunctional.

Brianna yawned, still feeling a bit lethargic. Shifting in bed to her side, she decided to do just like Cash had told her to do and take a nap. He liked giving orders. He liked making demands. She smiled, thinking that she liked him.

As she closed her eyes, her mind was filled with Cash.

Sixteen

It was Monday morning.

Cash glanced at his watch as he stood on the porch in the exact location where he'd stood on Friday. Like then, he was expecting Brianna to arrive any minute. However, today her arrival meant something else as well. He was anticipating her answer to his marriage proposal.

Granted, she might not think of it as a real proposal since he hadn't gotten down on one knee, nor had he slid an engagement ring on her finger. He knew Brianna hadn't expected either. In fact, it was quite obvious she hadn't expected his counteroffer of marriage. But he had made it and he had no intention of withdrawing it.

He had no choice.

Little did she know that it had nothing to do with

the fifty acres like she assumed. His counterproposal came from his need to claim her as his wife, the mother of the children he hadn't even known he wanted.

It was obvious to him that not only had Alan Dawkins betrayed her, he had failed to do right by her in the bedroom as well. Both were bad, but the latter was inexcusable. Cash's goal, for as long as it took, was to get her to see, and accept, that she was worthy of a man's respect.

When he had returned to her place on Saturday with food that he'd gotten from a restaurant in town, she was still sleeping. Chances were she hadn't slept well the night before, and he figured he was partly to blame for that. There was no doubt in his mind that his counteroffer had thrown her for a loop, and he'd not given her much time to answer him.

That part had been intentional.

As a businessman he knew not to give an opponent too much time to make a decision. Overthinking anything could cause problems and unnecessary delays. Delays he didn't want.

Brianna didn't have a clue as to the extent of his desire for her. There was more going on between them than a sexual attraction, even if he couldn't name what it was. That was the real reason he'd made the counteroffer for marriage. Point blank, he couldn't imagine any other man making her his.

On Saturday he hadn't bothered waking her. He had left the food on her table with a note that he would see her Monday morning. He wanted to give her time by herself to make her decision without any influence from him. He just hoped she made the right one.

* * *

Brianna saw Cash the moment she pulled into the long driveway of the Blazing Frontier. Butterflies were going off in her stomach. She knew what her answer would be.

She'd never wanted to get married after the pain and humiliation Alan had caused. Therefore, her decision should have been a no-brainer. But all it had taken was to wake up Saturday after her nap to find the food Cash had brought to her along with the note he'd left. Then to think about the relationship they'd shared over the past two weeks. The sexual chemistry had been there from day one, but he certainly wasn't the obnoxious type. Cash Outlaw in the flesh was everything she had fancied him to be when he'd been her fantasy boyfriend.

Now she had decided to make him her in-the-flesh husband. She would be entering this marriage with blinders off. She would get what she wanted—a baby—and Cash would get what he wanted—her fifty acres. They would both be happy. Besides, he'd given her another incentive. Marrying him would make her co-owner of the Blazing Frontier. In a way she felt good knowing that her child's…*their* child's…future would be secure.

Now if she could only accept his way of wanting to make a baby. After what happened on Saturday, she wasn't certain sharing a bed with Cash would be wise. There was no doubt it would be pleasurable, but the last thing she wanted to do was let off-the-charts sex take over her common sense.

If a kiss could make her feel the way she had on

Saturday, she didn't want to imagine what making love with him would do. Unfortunately, she *was* imagining, even those times when she did not want to do so. Like now. Seeing him standing on the porch in such a sexy pose while drinking a cup of coffee was stirring her blood.

When she brought the car to a stop and got out, she saw the smile that curved his lips. A smile that made her insides feel like mush. "Good morning, Cash."

"Good morning, Brianna."

He always said her name in a deep, husky tone. Today, his voice sounded even huskier. "I hope you have a cup of coffee for me," she said as she stepped up on the porch to stand in front of him.

"I've got something better than that. I went back to that café and grabbed breakfast. I hope you're hungry."

She was, and when she saw his mouth move—the mouth that had given her so much pleasure Saturday—she had to force air into her lungs. "Yes, I'm hungry."

"Good." He opened the door, and she followed him into the kitchen. "Go ahead and have a seat at the table and I'll warm everything up for you."

"Thanks."

First he poured her coffee, and she was glad of that because she needed it. Then she settled in the chair and watched him move around the kitchen, appreciating—as she always did—how he looked in his jeans. Today he was wearing a T-shirt that showed the muscles of his upper arms and tight abs.

The aroma of what he was warming up flowed over to her. "Strawberry muffins."

He chuckled. "Yes."

Moments later he placed the warm plate of muffins in front of her and took his seat. They began eating in silence. "How was the rest of your weekend?"

She shrugged. "Quiet." No need to tell him that she hadn't ridden Baby yesterday for fear of running into him again if she ventured off her property. "What about your weekend?" she asked, knowing they were stalling to avoid what was really on both their minds.

"Yesterday I decided to go through more of that stuff in the attic. I missed having you there working alongside me."

Brianna didn't say anything because they never really worked alongside each other even when she was there. That would have been too close for comfort, but she knew what he meant. He had missed her yesterday. That was good to know.

They continued to eat with little conversation, but she knew he was watching her. She dared not glance up and catch him staring.

"Brianna?"

She looked over at him, certain what he wanted to know. They had stalled long enough. "Yes?"

"What is your decision?"

Brianna drew in a deep breath as she placed her coffee cup down and met his gaze. Just staring into his eyes made her pulse rate increase.

"Yes, I will marry you, Cash."

Seventeen

Cash released the breath he'd been holding. He was getting the marriage he wanted. He stared at Brianna, wishing desperately he could read her thoughts to determine her true feelings about the decision she had made.

He wanted to ask her if she was sure, but he wasn't certain he wanted to hear what she might say. In time he would prove to her that marrying him was the right thing to do and he intended to make her happy or die trying.

Now, with her decision made, he wouldn't waste time. Before he could broach the subject, she said, "However, I prefer we wait a couple of weeks, even a month, before we marry."

"Why?"

"I need time to adjust to the idea."

Cash thought any adjustment time she needed could be done while married to him. "I told you I wanted to get married within forty-eight hours and I meant it, Brianna. I won't change my mind on that. I checked and there's no waiting period in Wyoming."

"What's the rush?"

"I need to secure my investors and get things moving around here." Honestly, that was the least of his concerns, but he wouldn't tell her that. "We're getting married Wednesday."

"Wednesday?"

"Yes. That will give you time to do whatever you need to do before then. In fact, I suggest we take the rest of the day off here. That will give you even more time. If you prefer, I'll make all the arrangements."

Brianna gave him an irritated look. "Fine, make all the arrangements."

She began nibbling on her bottom lip and he knew something was bothering her. "Is there anything else, Brianna?"

"I suggest that we marry someplace other than Black Crow."

He figured she had her reasons for making that suggestion. It really didn't matter where they got married, as long as they did so, legal and binding. "What about Jackson? I can fly us there in my plane."

He saw relief in her eyes. "Jackson will be fine."

"And be prepared to stay until Sunday."

Her expression showed that she was surprised by his request. "Until Sunday? Why?"

"A honeymoon. I want one, although it will be rather short. We'll take a longer one later."

"We don't have to take one now or later. It's not as if it's a real marriage."

Was now the time to discuss just how real he wanted their marriage to be? She would find out soon enough. "It's the only one I ever intend to have, Brianna, so let's make plans to stay in Jackson until Sunday."

"Whatever." She stood to take her plate to the sink and rinsed it out to place in the dishwasher. He saw her tense when he carried his own plate to the sink and stood beside her. "I don't bite, Brianna. Why are you acting so skittish today?"

"I'm not acting skittish."

"Yes, you are."

She turned to him. "If I am, then it's because I've agreed to do something that I swore I would never do."

He reached out and touched her cheek, feeling her emotions in every word. "I'm not a bad guy, and you do want the best for our child, right?"

"Yes."

"Then I'm asking you to believe I will do right by you both." He paused a moment, then asked, "Do you trust Henry Cavanaugh's office to keep things confidential?"

She lifted a brow. "Mr. Cavanaugh will, but Lois Inglese won't. She's been known to talk. I figured that's how word got out that Ms. Ellen had a son days before you showed up for the signing of the will."

Cash frowned. "Why does he keep her on?"

"She's worked there for years. He has counseled her about loose lips but I'm not sure how well that has worked. Why?"

"I want you to know I will do right by you, and

I'm having my cousin draw up a legal document to that effect."

"Your cousin?"

"Yes, Jared Westmoreland. He practices family law. I suggest you consult your own attorney to review everything with you before Wednesday."

"I can take the document to Mr. Cavanaugh as a consultation without him keeping a copy on file. That way there will be no need for Lois to see it."

Cash nodded. "Okay, then. I will get the document to you."

Brianna grabbed the mail out of her mailbox before entering her home. She had called Mr. Cavanaugh's office to make an appointment for tomorrow morning. Cash had assured her his cousin would be faxing the documents over to her by three this afternoon.

Drawing in a deep breath, she tossed the mail on the coffee table before dropping down on the sofa. She wanted to believe that being married to Cash would be okay. He would be spending the majority of his time in Alaska. If anyone asked her about her husband's long and periodic absences, she would merely tell them he had a business to run in Alaska and she was in charge of their operations at the ranch. At least during his visits his child would get to know him. She was comforted to know he'd have a part-time dad rather than not having one at all.

Brianna stood. She had a lot to do by Wednesday. Taking out her phone, she began making calls and setting appointments. Her hair needed to be done, and she would get a manicure and pedicure.

She had finished making her calls and was about to pick up her mail and go through it when her cell phone rang. It was Cash. "Yes?"

"I just talked to Jared. His office will be faxing the documents to you in a few minutes."

"Okay."

"And I've made all the arrangements with the airport. I will pick you up Wednesday morning around seven."

"I'll be ready."

When she ended the call, she glanced at her watch. It wasn't yet noon, but she needed to get away. Since she had so many appointments lined up tomorrow, now would be a good time to drive to Laramie to shop for several outfits and items.

If she went shopping in town for the clothing she needed, someone would speculate as to why. The last thing she wanted was for anyone to get into her business. They would find out soon enough.

"You're marrying Brianna?"

Cash heard the disbelief in Garth's voice. "Yes, I'm marrying her."

"Please don't tell me you're doing so because of those fifty acres."

Cash rubbed his hand down his face, knowing he could BS answers with Sloan and Maverick, but when it came to Garth and Jess, Cash never had such luxury. They could read him like a book each and every time.

"I had something she wanted, and she had something I wanted, so we agreed to compromise."

"By getting married?"

"Yes, by getting married."

Cash knew his brother was trying to take it all in. It didn't take Garth long to ask, "When will the wedding take place?"

"We're eloping."

"To Vegas?"

"No, to Jackson, Wyoming. Like Nevada, there's no delay in getting married in Wyoming. We're applying for the license on Wednesday morning and will get married that evening."

"No honeymoon?"

"There *will* be a honeymoon. We won't return to the ranch until Sunday. I know I said that I would be in the office on Monday and I still plan to be."

"You're bringing Brianna back with you?"

"No."

"You're moving to Black Crow?"

"Not at first."

"The two of you plan to have a long-distance marriage?" Garth then wanted to know.

Cash eased off the sofa, went to the window and looked out. The sun would be going down in a few hours and he wanted to ride the range before it did. "Such an arrangement will work for us."

"You think so?" Garth asked.

"You don't?" Cash countered.

"No. I watched you with her, Cash. I also know the reason you went early to Wyoming and why you stayed behind had everything to do with Brianna Banks. She has come to mean a lot to you. I would suggest you accept that." He paused. "Maybe you already have."

Knowing it was time to end the call, Cash said, "I'd

appreciate it if you don't mention my plans to anyone, especially Bart. I'll tell everyone when I return home next week. That's when I'll let them know it's a deal with the Blazing Frontier becoming a horse ranch as well as being a dude ranch again."

A couple hours later, Cash returned to the ranch house after going riding. There was something about this place that renewed his energy. Made him feel as if he was in his element. He was honestly getting used to the place, but he knew he would get even more used to it when he was here with Brianna as his wife.

Eighteen

"Are you sure you packed everything you're going to need, Brie?"

Brianna smiled as she moved around her bedroom. It was Wednesday morning and Cash would be arriving in less than an hour. "Yes, Miesha. I packed last night. I'm just putting together my toiletries and makeup."

"Your dress is beautiful."

A few minutes ago she had taken a picture of the dress and sent it to Miesha over the phone. "Thanks. You don't think it's too fancy, do you?"

"No. I think it will look beautiful on you. I wish I could be there with you today."

"I wish you could, too, but like I said, it's not that kind of ceremony. You know after Alan I never intended to get married anyway, so I don't plan to make a big deal of it."

"Regardless of what you might not have planned, you should be happy if for no other reason than knowing you'll get the baby you wanted."

Brianna knew that to be true. "Hopefully you and Darrett can come visit this summer once we get the dude ranch up and running again."

"Trust me, we will. He's fascinated with horses so maybe he can learn to ride while we're there. That has to make you feel good, knowing Cash is putting you in charge of everything."

Brianna paused what she was doing and drew in a deep breath. Cash had given her everything he'd promised in the documents that he had faxed to her. She would be co-owner of the Blazing Frontier while they were married.

There were a number of other things he had included that she hadn't expected, and Mr. Cavanaugh had concluded that her husband-to-be had been very generous and there was no reason she should not sign the documents. She had signed them and had faxed them back already.

"I know you packed a lot of sexy stuff, right?"

Brianna laughed. "I packed enough."

"Are you ready for Cash Outlaw to rock your world?"

She hadn't told Miesha what happened on Saturday and how he had not only rocked her world, he had literally made her weak in the knees. "As prepared as I'll ever be, I guess." She then glanced at the clock. "I need to get off the phone and finish doing everything.

I've been so busy I haven't even read the mail. I figure most of it is junk anyway since I pay the majority of my bills online."

"Enjoy your day, Brianna. You might be lucky and get pregnant tonight."

"I wish."

"Then that will be my wish for you, too."

After ending the call, Brianna watered her plants. Ted would be taking care of Baby while she was gone and she appreciated it. She glanced at her watch. Cash would be arriving any minute. Moving to her fireplace, she looked up at the picture hanging there of her parents. Seeing them together and knowing how much they'd loved each other gave her the will to make it through today and believe everything would work out alright.

When she heard a car pull up outside, she knew Cash had arrived.

"This is nice, Cash," Brianna said as they boarded the small plane.

"Thanks." He tried not to stare at her, but from the moment he had picked her up he couldn't keep his eyes off her. Her hair was different, styled in a way that complemented her features. He had told her more than once how much he liked it.

The flight from Laramie to Jackson went smoothly. Brianna sat beside him in the cockpit, although she slept most of the way there. He figured she hadn't gotten a lot of sleep the night before, and if he had his way, she wouldn't get much sleep tonight either.

It would be their wedding night.

She woke up when he landed the plane, and she quickly sat up and glanced around. "We're here?"

He smiled over at her. "Yes, we are here."

Cash had made all the arrangements for the day. Once they left the airport in a rental car that he had reserved for them, they stopped for breakfast before driving to the courthouse to get a marriage license. Surprisingly, the process took less than thirty minutes. Then he drove them to the hotel after informing Brianna the wedding ceremony would take place at five o'clock in a chapel not far away.

The hotel was beautiful, a five-star, and they had connecting rooms. Glancing around her suite, Brianna was truly impressed. It was huge, larger than most studio apartments, and beautifully decorated. What she truly liked was the separate living areas. She could dress for the ceremony in her own space.

She saw no reason to unpack since Cash had said they wouldn't be spending the night here. After the ceremony they would leave for Jackson Hole, a section of Jackson that was a valley between the Teton Mountain Range and the Gros Ventre Range.

Jackson Hole was known as a place where celebrities and those persons with plenty of money to spend migrated for fun and enjoyment. She and Cash would be there for a three-day honeymoon of sorts. At least, he was referring to it as that. She only thought of it as baby-making time.

She checked her watch and saw it wasn't quite noon but close to it. Since Cash hadn't mentioned anything about lunch, she figured he intended for this to be a do-your-own-thing time, which was fine with her. She needed all the time possible before the ceremony to think about how her life would be changing.

Then again, maybe it was better if she didn't think about it at all.

The more she thought about it the more apprehensive she got, and it was too late to get cold feet now. For a woman who'd always dreamed of a fairy-tale wedding day, this certainly wasn't how she'd thought it would be. But then, Alan had destroyed a lot of things for her, when she thought of the time spent planning their wedding, sending invitations. Luckily, she hadn't had any wedding gifts to return.

Sighing deeply, she decided not to look back but to look ahead. The thought of one day holding a child in her arms—her child—would be worth working through any misgivings she had.

She'd walked to her luggage to pull out something that was more comfortable to put on, when her cell phone rang. It was Cash. She had given him a special ringtone.

"Yes, Cash?"

"I'm going downstairs to grab lunch. Would you like to join me?"

"No, thanks." No need to tell him she was too nervous to eat right now. "I'm still full from breakfast. If I get hungry later, I'll order room service."

"Okay. And just so you know, I have plans for dinner after the ceremony."

"Oh? Where?" she asked him.

"It's a surprise."

She would rather it not be, but instead she said, "Alright. I'll wait for the surprise."

"You won't be disappointed. I'll see you at the chapel at five."

Another thing he had told her was that he had made arrangements for them to arrive at the chapel separately. He wanted to get there early to make sure everything was as he'd requested. A private car would be picking her up around four thirty.

Although she knew they would be spending a few days in Jackson Hole, she had no idea where. She had only herself to blame for not knowing any details since she had passed all the marriage arrangements to Cash. It would appear rather petty of her to question anything now.

She figured she would grab an hour of sleep before she showered and got ready. She really wasn't sleepy since she had slept on the plane, but she was getting antsy and needed to calm her nerves. Just the thought that this was her wedding day—and then to think about the wedding night—was enough to make her heart beat too fast.

She had kicked off her shoes and slid half out of her jeans when there was a knock on her door. She quickly pulled her jeans back up and wondered if that was Cash. Did he think she had changed her mind about lunch?

After giving herself a quick look in the mirror and fluffing her hair back from her face, she moved toward the door. Pausing, she glanced through the peephole and nearly screamed. Then she could not open the door fast enough.

"Surprise!"

"Miesha!" Brianna exclaimed, pulling her best

friend into the hotel room. "What on earth? What are you doing here? How did you know where I was? You didn't tell me you would be here. You had me send you a picture of my dress and everything, and you didn't say a word."

Miesha laughed. "Cash arranged everything. He contacted me yesterday morning at my office and invited me, but told me not to say anything to you about it. He wanted it to be a surprise."

Brianna couldn't help but grin as she and Miesha sat down on the sofa. "But how did Cash get your number?"

"He said you told him my name and the type of business I owned, and he looked me up on Google. Girl, I was totally surprised. He was so thoughtful to want to have me here with you."

Brianna couldn't believe it. "All this time Cash had me thinking it would be a small and private wedding with just me and him. Now I wonder if his brothers will be attending."

"Just his oldest brother, Garth, and Garth's wife, Regan."

Brianna tilted her head to look at Miesha. "How do you know?"

Miesha smiled. "Because Cash not only invited me to the wedding, but he provided transportation to get here. Garth's wife is their company pilot. She and Garth flew the company jet to Atlanta and picked me up and then we flew here. I thought it was cute how they took turns piloting the plane. They are super nice people. You're getting great in-laws."

Brianna nodded. She had met Cash's brothers and

was looking forward to meeting Garth's wife. "It doesn't matter how nice my in-laws are. You know as well as anyone that Cash and I won't have a real marriage."

"Well, evidently his brother and sister-in-law didn't get that memo. They are excited about the wedding. So am I, and I'm here to be with you. Darrett is with my folks."

"Are you staying at this hotel?"

"Yes. My bedroom is across the hall. Garth and Regan's room is also on this floor, but down the hall. They will fly me back home tomorrow, then fly to Florida to visit Regan's father. Garth said his other brothers don't know about the wedding. Cash wants to tell them himself when he returns to Alaska next week."

Brianna thought about everything Miesha had just told her. Cash was putting more into their wedding than she had expected him to. Just the idea that he'd made arrangements for Miesha to be here with her was special.

"What are you thinking about, Brianna?"

She met her best friend's gaze and said, "Cash is making it hard for me not to love him."

"But you do love him."

Brianna lifted her brow. "I never told you that."

Miesha's smiled. "You didn't have to, Brie. I could hear it in your voice, and I know that voice. I heard that same excitement when you returned to college that fall telling me all about your fantasy boyfriend."

"You know why, Miesha."

"Yes. Cash replaced Alan in your mind that summer and it worked. In fact, I think you fell in love with him then, Brie."

Recently Brianna had begun thinking the same thing.

Miesha glanced at her watch. "Come on. Let's grab lunch. Garth introduced me to Cash in the lobby when we first arrived. Definitely eye candy, girlfriend. He was on his way out, said he had to pick a few things up." She chuckled. "I heard he even hired a photographer so you'll have memories of today. Cash Outlaw is really taking this wedding seriously. He is trying to make sure today is special for you."

"It definitely seems that way," Brianna said thoughtfully.

"Cash also told me you hadn't eaten anything since breakfast. The last thing I want is for you to pass out from hunger during the wedding ceremony."

Brianna didn't want it to happen either. Standing, she grabbed her purse off the table. "Okay, let's go."

Nineteen

Cash knew the moment Brianna walked into the chapel. He had been talking to Garth and when he turned, she was there, standing in the doorway with her best friend, Miesha, and Garth's wife, Regan. Garth had mentioned that Regan had gone to Brianna's hotel room and introduced herself, to see if she needed help with anything.

He felt a sudden tightness in his throat when his gaze roamed over her. She looked amazing, beautiful. She was wearing a pink silk dress. It stopped at her knees with a beautiful lace hem border. He remembered once telling her how much he liked the color pink on her. Had she worn the color just for him? Pink made her appear feminine and sexy. The color also enhanced her complexion as well as highlighted the darkness of her eyes.

She wore a pair of silver stilettos, which looked to have a four-inch heel. He'd never seen her in heels that high and they enriched the beauty of a gorgeous pair of legs. When she began nibbling on her bottom lip, he knew she was nervous, probably from him staring so hard. But he couldn't help it. His heart began beating nearly uncontrollably. Brianna Banks was his.

"Are you going to just stand here and stare or are you going to claim your bride to get this wedding underway?"

Cash glanced back at his brother. "I am claiming my bride."

He walked off toward Brianna, holding her gaze with every step he took. Coming to a stop in front of the three women, he noticed Garth had walked over with him and stood by his side. "Regan. Miesha," Cash greeted the two women. He then glanced at Brianna. "You look beautiful."

She seemed to blush. "Thanks."

Offering her his arm, he said, "Let me introduce you to Reverend Epps."

In less than five minutes, Cash and Brianna were facing each other in the chapel. He had hired someone to decorate it and she had said she liked it. She also said she liked the bridal bouquet of hollyhocks he had presented to her. One day while out riding she had mentioned her favorite flower was hollyhocks and he had remembered.

Garth was his best man and Miesha was her maid of honor. She'd obviously asked Regan to be her attendant. When Reverend Epps told them to hold hands, he reached for Brianna's hand and felt her tremble. She tilted her head up to meet his gaze as they followed the minister's instructions and spoke their vows.

The words flowed from his lips freely and her responses were clear as she continued to hold his gaze. He took that as a positive sign.

"By the powers invested in me by the great state of Wyoming, I now pronounce you husband and wife. Mr. Outlaw, you may kiss your bride."

Cash smiled when he saw apprehension in her features. He knew as well as she did that their kisses could take on a life of their own. He winked to let her know he wouldn't do anything to give the minister heart palpitations, and Garth a reason to jab an arm in his ribs.

He wrapped his arms around Brianna's waist, leaned in and captured her lips in a kiss that wasn't chaste, nor was it as hot and greedy as he could have made it. Those kinds of kisses would come later.

Upon releasing her mouth, he smiled at her. Then the minister beamed his approval and said, "Congratulations, Mr. and Mrs. Cash Outlaw. I wish the two of you the very best, and may you have a long and happy life together."

Without breaking eye contact with Brianna when he replied to the minister, Cash said, "Thank you, Reverend Epps. I'm going to make sure of it."

More words of congratulations came from Garth and Regan and of course Miesha, who was shedding happy tears. Brianna still couldn't believe her best friend was here and that Cash had made it happen. Regan had shown up at her hotel door, introducing herself and offering to do whatever she could to make Brianna's day special.

Brianna had liked Regan immediately and she could see how Garth had fallen in love with her. There was no doubt in Brianna's mind it was a love match. She had seen the look in Garth's eyes the moment his wife had arrived at the church.

Brianna had also seen the look in Cash's eyes when he had seen her. She knew it had been lust and not love, but she would take it.

The photographer had taken a ton of pictures and she was glad. She would need them to convince herself she was truly married. Especially those times when he left her for days, for months, and she waited in Wyoming for his return.

She felt Cash's arms slide around her waist seconds before he leaned down and whispered, "It's time for us to go. We have reservations for dinner at six."

Nodding, she gave everyone hugs and waved goodbye. Cash then took her hand in his as they walked out of the chapel. She remembered her luggage was in the private car that had transported her, Miesha and Regan to the chapel. She glanced around for the car.

"What are you looking for?" Cash asked her.

"That private car with my luggage. I don't see it."

"The driver has taken our things on to Jackson Hole. Your luggage, as well as mine, should be in our room when we arrive after dinner."

Our room.

His reminder that they would be sharing a bed tonight sent shivers through her. Mistaking the shivers as a sign she was cold, he wrapped his arms around her shoulders and led her to the car.

He opened the car door for her and as soon as she slid onto the seat and snapped her seat belt in place, questions formed in her mind about just what the night held in store. Would it be anything close to the fantasies she'd had of him?

That kiss on Saturday had pretty much proven he would use his mouth in ways that should be forbidden. Even now when they were both seated in the car and he was about to start the engine, she could feel his sensual heat. Was such a thing normal? She wasn't sure because it hadn't happened to her with any other man, but then, Cash had been the first for her in many ways.

"The ceremony was nice, Cash. Thanks for arranging everything. I am especially grateful that you thought to have Miesha here. That was special."

"You are special."

Brianna wished she could believe he really thought that, and he wasn't just getting caught up in anticipation of a lustful night. Either way, she owed him a response. "Thank you. I think you are special, too."

The car had come to a traffic light, and he looked at her and smiled. He then reached out and took her hand in his and carried it to his lips. "Then I guess we are two special people who were meant for each other."

She was about to set him straight and tell him that it wasn't necessary to lay the compliments on so thick, then decided to just go with the flow. Besides, whenever he looked at her like that, she wasn't capable of setting him straight on anything.

"We're here."

Already? She glanced out the window at the extravagant restaurant. Although she hadn't ever eaten here, she had heard about it. The Jagged Edge was a popular place in Jackson that catered to an elite and extravagant crowd. She was neither, so she'd never put this place on her radar to visit.

A valet parked their car, and a smiling maître d' met them at the door. "Mr. and Mrs. Outlaw, congratulations. Your table is ready."

Brianna was surprised by the man's words. "You know him?" she asked Cash, trying to ignore the warmth of his hand at her back as they followed the man. The restaurant was huge and impressive, especially the triple stairs that led to other dining areas. The top was a cathedral ceiling with the largest chandeliers Brianna had ever seen. The back wall was completely glass to take advantage of the view of the lake.

"No, I don't know him personally. However, we met yesterday when I flew in to make all the arrangements."

He'd flown here yesterday? What kind of arrangements required him to come here in person? She got her answer the moment the maître d' opened the door to a private room.

Like the church, it was decorated with balloons and a banner that said Best Wishes Cash and Brianna. In the middle of the candlelit room was a table set for two with a beautiful view of the lake as a backdrop. A bottle of champagne was in a bucket, and soft music was playing.

"This is our own private wedding reception," he said, leading her to the table. "We will have an official one later where we can invite family and friends."

We will? That was news to Brianna, but she was too caught up with how beautiful the room looked to dwell on it now. She hadn't expected this. But then, she hadn't expected Miesha to be there for her either. Cash Outlaw was definitely full of surprises. Overcome with emotion, she had to struggle to collect herself before saying, "I hadn't expected any of this, Cash."

"I wanted to make things as special as you are, Brianna."

If he was working for brownie points, then he was doing a good job of getting them. "Thanks."

When they sat down, he grabbed the champagne bottle out of the bucket, opened it and poured some into their glasses. He lifted the glass in a toast. "To my beautiful wife."

She drew in a deep breath before she took her sip. Knowing she needed to add to the moment, she lifted her glass and said, "To my very thoughtful, kind and handsome husband."

After clinking their glasses, he threw his head back and laughed before taking a sip of his champagne. "You are laying it on rather thick, Brianna."

She smiled sweetly at him. "No more than you, Cash."

It seemed as if he would argue that point. Then, as if he thought better of it, he said, "I took the liberty of preordering our meal. I hope you don't mind."

"No, I don't mind." She was too nervous to study a menu anyway.

"I know how much you like salmon, and they have a superb dish that's baked with steamed carrots and pears over a white wine sauce."

"Sounds delicious."

"I had a sample tasting yesterday."

The waiter came with their meal. It looked pretty on their plates and she bet it was just as delicious. He had ordered the same thing for himself. Before leaving, the waiter poured more champagne into their glasses.

Over dinner she told him she had never learned to ski. He had informed her that since Jackson Hole was known for some of the best ski slopes, he intended to teach her. He didn't tell her much else about where they would be staying in Jackson Hole, and she figured she would have to wait to see it. He had said it was not a hotel, though.

When the music in the room seemed to get a little louder, Cash glanced at his watch. "Right on time. I instructed them that after we completed our meal, I wanted at least one dance with my wife before we left."

His wife...

Why did she feel a tingling sensation all through her body whenever he referred to her that way? She tilted her head up when he stood beside her chair and offered her his hand. "May I have this dance, Mrs. Outlaw?"

Mrs. Outlaw... Hearing him call her that made goose bumps form on her arms. Made her breath nearly catch. She stood and took his hand, and the moment they touched, a jolt of sexual energy passed between them. He tightened his hold on her as he led her to a shadowy section of the room.

Cash drew her into his arms, and as if it was the most natural thing, she went there without any hesitation. Resting her head on his chest, she got caught up in the sound of the soft romantic music that was playing while their bodies swayed.

It felt good being held in his arms as they slowly moved in rhythm. Blood rushed through her veins and her pulse rate increased.

Suddenly Cash stopped, although the music continued to play. She lifted her head from his chest to look up at him. Even in the semi-darkened room, she could see into his eyes from the moonlight shining off the lake.

She knew what was coming next and welcomed it. When he lowered his head, she tilted her chin up to meet his mouth. The connection fired her blood, made her heart rate kick up even higher, made her purr.

Only Cash could elicit such a response from her. He could do what others had failed to do. Although she had tried to deny it, she would admit now that this was the man she wanted, not just to father her child, but to be a part of her life.

At nineteen he had been her fantasy boyfriend, the man she had always wanted. Now he was her real husband.

He deepened the kiss and she let him. Cash had a way of breaking through her guard walls, lowering her defenses. Miesha had been right. Brianna needed to take charge, not let him be a drop-in husband. What she needed to do was use the days they spent together to give him a reason to visit her in Wyoming every chance he got. Could she pull off such a thing with her limited experience? She would certainly try.

He broke off the kiss and whispered against her moist lips, "It's time for us to leave."

Yes, he was right. It was time to leave. "Alright."

She was ready to act on the intense heat blazing between them.

Twenty

"This villa is beautiful, Cash."

Cash leaned against the closed door and watched as Brianna stood in the middle of the living room. As a romantic gesture he had carried her over the threshold and doubted he would ever forget the look of surprise on her face when he'd done so.

There was still a little daylight outside, so they had seen the beauty of the area when he'd driven across the scenic valley before crossing several snow-covered roads. The villa was at the top of one of the mountains in Jackson Hole.

It was part of a prestigious ski resort, and he had leased it for five days. This was one of their most secluded villas, and the two-story structure consisted of four bedrooms, three baths, a living room and a spacious eat-in kitchen. It was nestled among low-hanging trees, right by a huge lake with a view of much larger snowcapped mountains. There had been a drop in the temperature the higher he had driven up into the mountains.

"I'm glad you like it," he said, removing his tuxedo jacket and stepping away from the door to move toward her. "Did I tell you how beautiful you look?"

She nodded. "Yes, you told me."

"Everything about you today was perfect."

He meant it. She looked beautiful in pink. Her dress was exquisite, her makeup flawless and her hair—which was curled and pulled up with a bevy of ringlets around her face—made her look both serene and sexy.

More than once he had lost his train of thought while staring at her from across the dinner table. And at the wedding, while reciting his vows, he'd had to fight to retain his concentration. All he could think about was that by the end of the day, she would belong only to him. Not as a possession but as a treasure.

She didn't back up when he stopped in front of her. To him that was a good sign. Instead, she tilted her head back to meet his eyes while nervously licking her lips.

"Do you know what it does to me whenever I see you lick your lips like that, Brianna?"

She immediately stopped doing it. "No. What does it do to you?"

"It makes me want to be the one to lick them for you."

He saw the flash of heat in her eyes. Then, as if his words brought out a boldness in her, she deliberately licked them again, and whispered, "I welcome you to go for it, Cash."

That was all the invitation he needed. The moment their tongues touched, he had to fight for control. Brianna kissed him back with a need he felt all the way to his groin. Her response forced him to deepen the kiss. He wanted her to feel his hunger from the top of her head to the bottoms of her feet.

Her mouth tasted like the champagne they had consumed earlier. He wrapped his arms around her so tightly, he could feel the hardness of her nipples against his chest—nipples he had tasted once and looked forward to tasting again.

Knowing where this kiss would eventually lead and wanting them both naked when it did, he broke away and slowly lifted his head to stare down into her eyes. The intensity in the dark gaze staring back at him made his heart pound.

Drawing in a much-needed breath, he asked, "Do you want to get naked out here or in the bedroom?"

"In the bedroom," she said in a soft voice that fired up his libido even more.

Images of the two of them in bed, naked and making love, had him struggling for breath again. Without wasting any time, he swept her into his arms.

After Cash placed her on the bed and stepped back, Brianna could feel the intensity of his gaze as if it were a physical caress. She might not be experienced in some things, but at that moment, she was aware of the magnetism between them.

When he reached out his hand to her, she took it and

stood beside the bed with him. He released the clips holding her hair, making it flow around her shoulders. Then he reached behind her dress to slowly inch down the zipper.

Brianna forced breath through her lungs at the thought of Cash's hands touching her. These were the hands of her husband, the man she loved.

Yes, she loved him. Her love for him was absolute, even if he never felt the same. As long as he kept all the promises he'd made to her child, she could handle anything.

While holding her gaze, he stepped back and let the dress flow down her hips and land at her feet. His gaze went to her bra and this time he was the one who licked his lips. Seeing him do so reminded her of what happened the last time he'd enjoyed her breasts. The reminder made heat settle in the area between her legs.

Brianna had always liked matching bra and pantie sets, and while shopping in Laramie, she had purchased a few of them. The one she wore today was the exact shade of pink that matched her wedding dress.

"Thanks for making things easy for me," he said when his fingers went to the front clasp of her bra and removed it with the proficiency of a man who'd done so many times. That thought didn't bother her. She believed him when he'd said she would be the only woman he slept with now.

She watched when he knelt before her to inch the thong down her legs and suddenly, she felt bashful. No man had ever undressed her before, and Cash was taking his time doing so.

When she lifted her legs to step out of her thong,

she wondered why he hadn't removed her shoes first. She got her answer when he glanced up at her and said, "Seeing you naked in a pair of stilettos is a vision that will be branded into my mind forever. You look so hot and sexy. So damn desirable it makes me ache."

He was still down on his knees in front of her and she held his gaze. His words made every pulse point within her body come alive. Every inner muscle tightened. Her nipples hardened.

She knew he saw her reaction.

Then he grabbed her thighs and buried his head between her legs. When she felt his tongue invading her womanly core, she clutched his shoulders. Otherwise her knees would have given out on her, right then and there.

Using his tongue as a sensuous weapon, he dived deep inside of her, and she moaned at the intimate invasion. He drove his tongue even deeper and sucked harder, greedily, as if he loved her taste and couldn't get enough.

Alan had never done this to her, but she'd heard talk at college about guys doing this and what a mind-blower it was. Her friends were right. She wanted to scream for him to stop in one breath, and then beg for him to continue in the other. How could she feel so brazen to let a man do this to her?

But then, Cash wasn't just any man. He was her husband. Whatever she allowed him to do was fine. Then she felt his hands tighten on her thighs as he wiggled his tongue inside of her. She gave up fighting the sensations that took over her mind and body.

Grabbing the back of his head, she tried pressing

him more intimately to her, wanting more of what he was doing. When she felt a sharp pleasure hit her just where his mouth was connected to her body, she screamed and fell backward on the bed as her legs gave out.

Cash didn't stop. He couldn't. His mouth remained clamped tight to her feminine mound, while his tongue drove even deeper inside of her. He loved her taste. He loved the sounds she was making and he loved her scent.

Brianna Outlaw.

Her name was now his.

He hoped they created their baby tonight. Not because she wanted a child, but because he wanted one, too. Suddenly, more than anything, he wanted a baby with Brianna.

When the last of the tremors finally left her body, he pulled his mouth from her, removed her shoes and readjusted her position on the bed before tackling the chore of removing his own clothes. Through a pair of exhausted eyes, she watched him.

He smiled at her. "Don't get sluggish on me now, sweetheart."

She looked totally sexy lying on her back, naked, with her legs slightly spread. Her eyes closed as she tried to regain control of her breathing. With each intake of air into her lungs, her breasts moved, and the sight of the darkened nipples was arousing.

She opened her eyes to look at him. "I honestly don't know if I have the energy for anything more, Cash," she said in a tone that he would have found con-

vincing had he not known better. Whether she knew
it or not, his wife was a passionate woman. That was
obvious in the way she returned his kisses.

"Trust me. You will find the energy."

Brianna looked skeptical, but he had a feeling
her body would be ready whenever his was. Even
now, there were signs of her vitality returning as
she watched him undress. He could see it in the eyes
watching his every move, the rise and fall of her chest
that denoted the heaviness of her breathing.

When he slid his tuxedo pants down his legs along
with his briefs and stood before her completely nude,
he even heard her purr.

"Your body is beautiful, Cash."

He smiled at the compliment. "Your body is beautiful, too. Are you ready for me, baby?"

Without taking her gaze off his midsection, she
nodded. "Yes, I'm ready."

Cash smiled, looking forward to teaching her all the
ways they would pleasure each other. "Good, because
I'm ready, too." He got back on the bed and slowly
eased up her body.

When he was in the right position, he stared down
at her and saw the intensity in the eyes staring back
at him. That look tempted him to lean in and kiss her.
She was his. He had gotten more than the marriage he
demanded. He had gotten the wife he desired.

He captured her mouth with his.

Brianna was convinced no man could kiss better
than Cash. He not only used his mouth and tongue to

bring her to an aroused state, but he also used them to push her close to the edge then snatch her back.

She moaned in protest when he finally released her mouth, and gazed up at him while trying to get her breathing back in sync. That's when she felt him nudge her legs apart with his knee. As he held her gaze, he slowly slid inside of her, stretching her body to accommodate him.

Sensations overtook her the deeper he went, and she couldn't stop the moans that slipped past her lips. "Cash…"

"I'm here, sweetheart." And then, as if to prove that he was, he held their joined hands above her head. That made her breasts lift with the nipples pointing at his mouth. She saw the fiery look in his eyes when he noticed as well.

Two things happened simultaneously. He leaned in and latched onto a nipple, easing it into his mouth, and her inner muscles—as if with a mind of their own—clamped down. It was as if they were trying to pull everything out of him.

That's when she heard his moan, but he didn't let go of the nipple in his mouth. While her body was milking him below, he was using the same technique on her breast. That realization sent shivers down her spine.

He released the nipple to gaze down at her as he moved, thrusting in and out, slowly at first. Making sure she felt every incredible inch of him. She wrapped her legs around him as his body began pounding her hard into the mattress, pushing her over the edge and making her scream his name.

And he screamed hers.

Not only did he scream her name, but she felt him let loose inside her. The very essence of him coated her insides. She screamed his name again when the sensations kept coming, kept tearing into her with a force she had never felt before. The violent tremors took her breath away.

Then the shudders slowed. The intensity of her pleasure made her whisper his name in admiration and awe. She hadn't known making love to someone could be like this. Overpowering. Satisfying. Full of contentment.

She felt drained, totally sapped. The last thing she recalled before drifting off was Cash kissing the side of her face, whispering for her to rest because there was more to come.

Daylight streaming in through the window brought Cash awake. He glanced around the room, knowing where he was and who he was with. There was no doubt in his mind whose legs were entwined with his and whose warm body he held in the spoon position.

My wife.

He smiled, liking the sound of that.

She was still asleep and he understood why. It had been one wild night. Brianna hadn't thought she had energy left for round two or three. She'd surprised herself.

Now Cash was glad he hadn't planned any activities for them today, other than eating and making love. He glanced at the clock. It was eight in the morning. He had ordered their breakfast to be delivered to their villa at nine. To ward off the cold, he started a blaze in the bedroom's fireplace. In no time, it was throwing off good heat in the room.

This was a beautiful villa. It was larger than what they needed, but he'd loved the layout when he'd seen it online. He had chosen this particular villa because of the location. He wanted complete privacy with Brianna. It wouldn't hurt his feelings any if they didn't see another human being for as long as they were here together.

Making love to her through the night had been one of the most pleasurable things he'd ever done. That had him wondering how he would handle those nights in Alaska when she would be in Wyoming. Hopefully he wouldn't have to. When he returned to Alaska next week, he had an idea he would run by Garth.

Brianna shifted in his arms and then slowly rolled over to face him. When their gazes connected, he felt a spark of renewed arousal and knew she felt it, too. There was no way she couldn't when his erection pressed hard against her.

"Good morning, Cash," she said in a soft voice.

"Good morning, Brianna. However, I believe the morning-after greeting should go something like this."

Then he kissed her. Finally releasing her mouth, he snuggled her closer.

"What's planned for today?" she asked him.

"Breakfast will be delivered at nine. Lunch at one. Dinner at six. Very good reviews on the food and service here."

"And in between lunch and dinner?"

He smiled. "For me it will be Brianna at ten, eleven

and twelve. Then again at two, three, four and five. Then the rest of the day after dinner."

She giggled. "Is that your way of letting me know you plan to pretty much keep me on my back?"

"Yes, I guess you could say that. Of course, you can request to put me on my back whenever you want."

She laughed. "Thanks for being so accommodating."

"You're welcome. I guess we need to get up and throw something on for breakfast. Or better yet, we can always eat in bed." That was an idea he rather liked.

"Either way is fine with me."

He was glad to hear that. "We have activities planned for tomorrow. We're taking a cable car tour of Mount Laver."

"Sounds like fun."

"Um," he said, leaning in and kissing her on the side of her neck, "not as much fun as staying inside the villa with you."

Then he straddled her body, knowing he needed to make love to her before he could possibly get his day started. And from the sound of her breathing, she was all in.

Good.

Twenty-One

"How did I do today?" Brianna asked Cash after taking a shower and putting on a comfortable maxi dress. She loved how the linen material felt on her skin. However, what she liked most was the front zipper that ran the length of the neckline to the hem. Easy on and easy off.

For the past two days, he had taught her how to ski. They had rented everything they needed, from clothing to equipment. Today was their last at the Jackson Hole ski resort and she was missing being here already.

Thursday had been a stay-in-bed day, but Friday and today they had gotten out so Cash could teach her how to ski. More than once, she had stared down at her hand to see the beautiful wedding ring he had placed there as proof they were truly married. She had never thought having a husband would be so much fun, both in and out of the bedroom.

"You did well, but you're not ready for the slopes yet," Cash said, grinning.

They were high up in the Wyoming mountains. It was cold and the snow was heavy and thick. Whenever they returned to the villa, the fireplaces had the inside all warm and toasty. She loved being here with Cash. Whenever she thought about all the things they had done together, all the ways they had pleasured each other in the bedroom, she got both bashful and giddy inside.

They would be returning to the ranch tomorrow, and then he would leave for Alaska before daybreak Monday morning. She couldn't help wondering when he would return. Would he miss her when they were apart?

On the drive from Black Crow to the Laramie airport, she had told him she would be going to the doctor next week to get a temperature kit. That way she would know the best times to get pregnant. She figured those would be the only times he would return. Until then…

Because she would be wearing her ring, it wouldn't be long before word of her marriage got around. This morning at breakfast he had surprised her when he said he wanted her to move into the ranch house and turn it into a home. She figured he wanted the place to feel like a home whenever he dropped in.

Since the wedding, not once had they talked about the reason for their marriage. Others probably assumed they were a newly wedded couple who were madly in love.

"Do you like this place, Brianna?"

She glanced over at him. He was sitting on the rug in front of the fireplace. It had become one of their favorite spots at night to unwind and sip glasses of wine. Huge pillows were placed all around—a comfortable place to sleep or even make love.

"Yes, I really like it. Thanks for bringing me here." She paused. "Ready for our glass of wine?"

He glanced up at her. "Yes, I'll get it."

"No, stay put. I will get it."

Cash smiled up at her. "Okay."

She returned a short while later with a tray carrying their glasses and a bottle of wine. Each day a different bottle had been delivered to the villa, compliments of the resort.

She placed the tray by him and then eased down in front of the fireplace beside him. "You did a good job arranging everything, Cash."

She meant it. In less than two days he had made all the wedding arrangements as well as the ones for their five-day honeymoon. Not only was the resort itself wonderful, but the service was excellent, especially the food.

"It was all for you, sweetheart," he said.

He was gently caressing her cheek while gazing into her eyes. It was during tender moments like these when he truly felt like her fantasy husband. He had a way of making her think he was sincere in everything he said and did. Even when he used terms of endearment, which he'd been doing a lot, they flowed naturally from his lips.

She watched him pour wine into their glasses and then he handed her one. He held up his. "Let's toast our last night here together. The days were great." His smile transformed into a sexy grin. "I especially enjoyed the nights."

She held up her glass and agreed. "Yes, especially the nights."

They stared at each other over the rims of their wineglasses as they leisurely sipped. He had told her she was a very passionate woman and she was beginning to believe him. Although certain parts of their lovemaking could still leave her weak, it was a satisfying feeling.

In just three nights Cash had shown her that no two sessions of lovemaking were the same. *You get out of it what you put into it, granted your partner isn't a selfish or inconsiderate bastard.* Those were his words, not hers. Her excuse was that she and Alan had both been young and inexperienced.

As they continued to stare into each other's eyes, she could feel the sexual energy flowing between them. There was a buildup of need and desire slowly overtaking them. He was aroused, which was something a man couldn't hide. And their chemistry was more powerful than ever.

She knew Cash would soon act on all that hot, carnal awareness. However, tonight she intended to act first. Placing her wineglass aside, she stood. Knowing he watched her every move, she slowly lowered the zipper of her dress. If he had suspected she hadn't been wearing anything underneath, he knew it for certain now.

When she stood naked in front of him, she said, "Now for your clothes. Stand so I can take them off you." She was doing what she hadn't done yet—undressing him.

Brianna watched how he eased to his feet; even that was sexy. Without wasting any time, she moved to him and began unbuttoning his shirt, feeling the rapid beat of his heart against her fingers.

Next came his jeans, which proved to be difficult because of his aroused state. He took pity on her and helped her out. When he finally stood naked before her, she just stood there a moment looking at him. The firelight flickered across his body, making him look like a deep bronze Adonis.

She moved back toward him when he extended his arms to her. She went into them. "This is my night for you, Cash. One I want you to remember during your nights in Alaska without me."

She hadn't meant to say that, but now that she had, she didn't regret it. She wanted him to miss her. She wanted him to come back to her often. She wanted to have a purpose in his life that was more than the woman he had agreed to impregnate. The woman who had the land he wanted.

On tiptoe, she wrapped her arms around his neck, tempted at that moment to tell him that she loved him. However, she didn't feel brave enough for the words. She had said enough already.

So she kissed him.

She kissed him in all the ways he had taught her over the past few days. And when he kissed her back, she almost lost control of her senses. That was the last thing she wanted. Without knowing he'd done so, each and every time they had made love, Cash had branded her his. Now she wanted to brand him hers.

Without breaking their kiss, she began easing down to the floor with him, and then, when she did break off the kiss, she gently pushed him onto his back to straddle him.

She liked looking down at him, seeing the surprise in his eyes as well as the heat. There was something else there, too, a look she couldn't define. At that moment, he was as aware of her as she was of him.

When she deliberately lowered her midsection to rub her body against his, he moaned out her name.

"Brianna..."

"Yes?"

"Put me out of my misery."

He hadn't experienced her brand of misery yet. Instead of granting his request, she lowered her mouth to kiss him. Using the technique he had taught her, her tongue dueled with his.

When she broke off the kiss, she began kissing his chest, then moving lower to his stomach, and then she slid lower still. Before he could stop her, she had taken him into her mouth.

Cash was convinced Brianna was trying to kill him. He should have known he was a goner when she unzipped her dress to reveal her perfect body—beautiful shoulders, a pair of firm breasts with luscious nipples, a small waist, flat stomach, curvy hips and shapely legs.

The icing on the cake had been the dark triangle

at her center. It didn't matter that he had tasted her there and had gone inside of her every day since they'd married. Every time he saw her womanly mound, he wanted as much of it as he could get.

Cash let out a moan at the way Brianna was working her mouth on him. He grabbed her head, having a mind to make her stop. Instead of stopping her, he held her head right there as her mouth continued to greedily consume him.

He closed his eyes at the feel of her tongue wrapping around the head of his shaft. Nothing had prepared him for this. When she widened her mouth to take in the full length of his manhood, the bottom half of him nearly shot off the floor.

A growling sound escaped his lips, and when he felt his body getting ready to explode, he knew he wanted to be inside of her when it happened.

With all the strength he could muster, he grabbed hold of her shoulders and pulled her up over him. "I need to be inside of you. Now!"

He thrust upward and slid into her at the same time she came down on him. The connection was so intense, it shook them both. She then began moving up and down him, riding him hard.

He did upward thrusts and she did downward plunges. Together, the strokes intensified, electrified and nearly pushed them over the edge. It seemed neither was ready for this to end, so he deliberately snatched them back just to repeat the process over and over again.

Then Cash couldn't hold off any longer. When he exploded, it was so severe, it felt like it would shake his entire insides loose. From the trembling of her body, he knew she had felt the same thing. That's when he grabbed the back of her neck and brought her mouth down to his, and kissed her with a hunger that only intensified their orgasms.

It was only when the last shudders had left their bodies that he released her mouth and gathered her into his arms. They faced the fireplace to watch the flames and get their breathing under control.

Cash knew that leaving Brianna to return to Alaska would be the hardest thing he'd ever done, but now his trip home had a purpose. When he returned to Wyoming, he didn't intend to ever leave without her again.

Twenty-Two

"There you have it, Garth. Do you think it's a workable idea?"

Although the plan had been for Cash to return to the office for today's midday meeting, he'd honestly considered calling in to request more time off. After all, he had gotten married less than a week ago. But he'd needed to explain his idea to Garth in person.

Garth leaned back in his chair, nodding. "Yes, it's workable and a damn good idea. It would require the shifting of job duties between you, Sloan and Maverick, but I think they are ready for a change anyway. Sloan has hinted that he's getting tired of traveling so much. Now he can take over your duties here in the office."

Garth paused and then added, "And Maverick has been champing at the bit to work internationally for years. If we ever need you to attend an in-office meeting, your flight time between Wyoming and Alaska is less than five hours."

A huge smile spread across Cash's face. "Thanks." Setting up a satellite office of Outlaw Freight Lines in Black Crow, Wyoming, at the Blazing Frontier Ranch was a good idea. Cash would handle the company's expansion into various other states.

"So, when are you going to tell everyone that you're married?" Garth asked.

"After today's meeting. I plan to fly back to Wyoming tomorrow morning and then return with Brianna to introduce her to Dad over the weekend." Their father and Charm's mother, Claudia, had flown to see a Broadway show in New York and wouldn't be back until the end of the week.

"Just prepare yourself, and you might want to prepare Brianna. Bart still likes to think he's in control and calling the shots. He isn't going to like that you got married without consulting him first," Garth said.

Cash rolled his eyes. "I stopped consulting Bart about anything years ago. I usually take his advice with a grain of salt."

Garth chuckled. "Don't we all?"

Back in his office, Cash was glad things had turned out so well. Of course, Sloan and Maverick, although surprised to hear he'd gotten married, were happy for him since they liked Brianna. He hadn't told Charm because she hadn't attended the meeting. She would have to wait and hear it from him at the same time he told Bart.

He leaned back in his chair as he remembered how he had awakened at the ranch house before dawn that morning to make love to Brianna before he left. She hadn't asked when he would be returning, so when she saw him tomorrow, she would certainly be surprised. And there was no doubt in his mind she would be surprised to know he was staying.

He had called to let her know he had arrived safely in Alaska. She was still in bed and said she would make this a lazy Monday for her. She would arrive at her house later today to check on things and go through her mail. It was her plan to return to the ranch house to spend the night and then begin moving her stuff this week.

Cash liked the thought of knowing that when he arrived at the ranch early tomorrow morning, she would be there in his bed. Then he would be there to help her move her stuff to the ranch. It was her home now and he intended for them to live together as husband and wife. Any misgivings about how she would feel about it had come to an end when she had unintentionally whispered that she loved him before drifting off to sleep after they'd made love this morning. Chances were she wouldn't remember saying it, but he had definitely heard her.

Hearing the words had made him finally understand what he'd been feeling all this time, why he knew he had to make this move to Wyoming.

He loved his wife.

More than anything, he looked forward to having her back in his arms again.

Brianna had thrown the last of her clothes in the dryer and decided to take time to eat lunch. She would definitely be busy this week. Cash had asked that she move into the ranch house and she'd promised she would. That meant she would start moving her things a little at a time.

When they'd talked that morning, she had been tempted to ask him when he would return, but kept herself from doing so. She had known what their marriage arrangements would be when she'd agreed to marry him. Just because they'd had a wonderful time on their honeymoon, that didn't mean anything had changed—although she had tried her best to make sure he would miss her while he was in Alaska.

Leaving the laundry room, she saw all the mail stacked up on her kitchen table. It was mail she'd been too busy to look through before leaving for the wedding. Most was junk mail anyway.

Thirty minutes later she had tossed most of it away when she came across a letter addressed to her from the law firm of Denese, Fryson and Cohen in Los Angeles. She frowned. Why would a law firm be writing to her? And where had she seen the name of that firm before? For some reason, it sounded familiar.

She tore open the letter, and as she read what it said, intense anger consumed her. Cash was going to contest the will? When had he planned this? The letter was dated more than a week ago. Before she had agreed to marry him. It had been delivered Tuesday.

Was this plan B in case she had turned down his counteroffer of marriage on Monday? From what the letter said, it seemed he had already put a plan into motion to take her to court and contest Ms. Ellen's will, not just for the fifty acres but for everything his mother had left her. That included her house, and the thought had her fighting back tears.

How could she have been so wrong about him? How could she have let another man play her for a fool? Tears she couldn't hold back streamed down her face. Never again. Never again.

Cash glanced down at his cell phone when it rang and smiled when he saw it was Brianna. He clicked it on. "I was just thinking about you, sweetheart."

"Were you? Why? Did your attorney let you know he had jumped the gun in sending that letter since I *did* consent to marry you?"

Cash frowned. "What are you talking about?"

"I am talking about the letter I got from your attorneys, Denese, Fryson and Cohen, stating your plans to contest the will. I guess that was your plan B in case I decided not to marry you."

"I have no idea what you're talking about."

"Tell that to someone else, Cash. Just so you know, I plan to get my own attorney and file for a divorce. I refuse to stay married to a man I cannot trust." And then she hung up on him.

Cash sat there holding the phone, not believing the conversation that had just transpired. He had no idea what Brianna was talking about. He'd never dealt with any law firm by the name of Denese, Fryson and Cohen.

He tried calling her back, but she wouldn't answer. Damn! Getting up from his desk, he crossed the hall to Garth's office and barged in without knocking. Garth snatched his head up from the papers he'd been reading. When he saw the anger on Cash's face, he stood and asked, "Cash, what's wrong?"

Cash then told Garth what Brianna had told him. "Damn it, Garth, I've never even heard of that law firm."

Garth's jaw tightened. "I have. They used to be Dad's attorneys out of LA."

"Dad?"

"Yes, but I had no idea he still had them on retainer."

Cash's frown deepened as he rubbed the back of his neck. "I swear, Garth, if Dad is responsible for this, there will be hell to pay. How dare this firm send any document on my behalf when they don't represent me. I can't believe they would notify Brianna that I would be contesting Ellen's will."

"How soon are you leaving for Wyoming?" Garth asked his brother.

An angry Cash met his brother's gaze. "I'm leaving as soon as I can get my plane ready."

Around midnight, Brianna was awakened by pounding on her door. Turning on the lamp by her bed, she got up and slid into her robe. She had a sinking feeling who it was. A quick look out the peephole confirmed her suspicions.

"What do you want, Cash?"

"Open the door, Brianna. We need to talk."

"No. We have nothing to say to each other. Just go away."

She was about to return to her bedroom when he

began pounding on her door again. "I am not leaving, Brianna. Open the door."

Brianna drew in a deep breath. Before going to bed, she had talked to Miesha, and her best friend had found it hard to believe Cash would do such a thing. Brianna hadn't wanted to believe it either, but she had those attorneys' letter to prove it.

"Brianna!"

She could hear the anger in his voice. What did he have to be mad about? She was the one who'd been played for a fool. "We have nothing to say, Cash."

"Yes, we do. Now open the door."

Fine, they would get it all out, but there was nothing he could say that would make her forgive him. She opened the door and looked at him. He stood under the porch light, his features tight and brooding. He was wearing a business shirt and slacks. Had he come straight from his office?

"Please say what you have to say and leave, Cash," she told him, closing the door behind him when he entered her home.

"You are wrong about me, Brianna."

She crossed her arms over her chest and glared up at him. "I got the letter from your attorneys, Cash. Now I know the truth. You were going to take everything Ms. Ellen left me. You pretended to be fine with my inheritance, but deep down you resented it and didn't want me to have anything. You were going to toss me out of my home like Hal Sutherland planned to do. You are no better than him."

Her words seemed to have struck him. His eyes lit with even more anger. "I did not have those attorneys send that letter, Brianna. Why would I send a letter contesting the will when I planned to marry you?"

"It was a plan you put in place just in case I turned you down."

He shoved his hands into the pockets of his jeans. "I planned to marry you whether you turned me down on Monday or not. You would have been my wife regardless."

His words infuriated her. "Are you saying I would not have had a say in the matter?"

"No, what I am saying is that you would have eventually said yes because we're good together. Because I couldn't live without you. Because I would have convinced you how much I want you. How much I love you."

She backed up as if his words were a weapon. "You don't love me."

"I do love you. I love you as much as you love me, Brianna."

She lifted her chin. "What makes you think I love you?"

"You told me this morning before I left. You said it right after we climaxed together that last time and before you drifted off to sleep."

Had she? "What I said after sex means nothing now. I am filing for a divorce." She watched him rub his hand down his face as if he was agitated. Brianna cared less how he was feeling when her heart had been broken.

Cash looked straight at her and said, "That firm does not represent me and I did not have them send you that letter. However, I think I know who did."

"Who?"

"My father."

Her frown deepened. "Why would your father do such a thing?"

"Because Bart Outlaw thinks he has the right to control every situation. Even those that involve his grown-ass sons."

"You want me to believe your father would do something like that knowing you would eventually find out about it?"

"Yes, because in his mind, he honestly believes he's looking out for our best interests."

Brianna didn't say anything because what he'd told her was pretty much what Ms. Ellen had said about her ex-husband. Suddenly, Brianna remembered why the name of that law firm sounded familiar. "That same firm also sent Ms. Ellen letters when she tried reaching out to you."

Cash lifted a brow. "Ellen tried reaching out to me?"

"Yes, for years. That same firm would return her cards and letters, threatening to sue her if she continued to contact you. It's all in that packet I told you about in your bedroom. She even hired a private investigator to send her periodic reports on how you were doing, when you refused to have anything to do with her."

Cash frowned. "I didn't know she tried reaching out to me. I figured she was no different than my brothers' mothers. That she never wanted to have a connection to me."

"Well, you were wrong."

* * *

I have been wrong...

Cash didn't say anything as his mind absorbed what Brianna had said. She had told him about that packet weeks ago, but he had refused to look at it. Now he wished he had, and tonight he would, but first he needed to make sure Brianna believed him.

"It seems Bart's deceit is deeper than I thought."

"I don't understand why your father would want to keep you away from your mother."

"Like I said, he thinks he has the right to control every situation when it comes to his sons. He gives orders and expects us to obey, but we never do."

Cash remembered that time Bart didn't want to accept the Westmorelands as the Outlaws' kin even though they all favored. His sons hadn't gone along with that directive either.

He moved to stand in front of Brianna. "I meant it when I said I love you. I've probably loved you from the first. I did not have any attorneys send that letter. I knew nothing about it. You have to believe me, Brianna."

"You father didn't want us to be together?"

Cash shook his head. "It's not about you, since he had no idea how I felt about you. For Bart, it's about him believing I am getting cheated out of something he feels is rightfully mine." He paused. "I recall him saying something to that effect when I returned to Alaska after the reading of the will and mentioning Ellen had left parts of her land to you. He said then that he thought I should get all of it. My mistake was dismissing what he thought. I hadn't figured he would do what he did."

"Do you think you're being cheated out of something that is rightfully yours, Cash?"

He shook his head. "No. The land was Ellen's to do with as she pleased. I was honestly surprised she left me anything. At the time, I thought she hadn't wanted any dealings with me. That's why I didn't want to keep the land. I hadn't wanted anything from her."

"And now?"

"You are the reason I changed my mind about the ranch, about my mother. Falling in love with you was the clincher."

"You do love me? Honestly?"

He reached up and caressed her chin. "I do love you. Honestly. I want to see what's in that packet to find out the truth. But first, I need to know that you believe me, Brianna. That you still love me. That is what is most important to me now."

She met his gaze and nodded. "Yes, I believe you."

Cash released the breath he'd been holding. He hadn't wanted to imagine her not believing him. He pulled Brianna into his arms and captured her mouth with his. He needed this. He needed her. Moments later, when he broke off the kiss, he whispered against her moist lips, "I love you."

Teary eyes stared up at him when she said, "And I love you."

He swept her off her feet and headed to her bedroom.

Twenty-Three

"Yes, I'm okay, Garth, but I'll be a whole hell of a lot better after I confront Bart," Cash said. "It's bad enough he had that law firm send that letter to Brianna, but to discover Bart also used them to keep Ellen from being a part of my life is unacceptable."

"I agree. Are you still returning this weekend?"

"Yes, and I'm bringing my wife with me. What Bart did was unforgivable."

Cash, with Brianna by his side, had gone through the packet. He saw all the birthday cards Ellen had sent that the attorneys had returned, along with their letters threatening what they would do if she continued to reach out to him. He'd also seen the private investigator's periodic reports on him. It changed everything he thought he knew about his mother. It hurt to think of all the time they'd missed.

"I told the brothers what Bart did, and we support you," Garth said. "Bart was wrong."

"Yes, he was."

When Brianna came into the living room with a cup of coffee for him, Cash said to Garth, "I'll talk with you later. Brianna and I will be coming in on Friday. I don't want anyone to mention anything to Bart."

After hanging up, Cash took the coffee cup Brianna offered him. After taking a sip, he put it aside to pull her into his lap. Seeing those cards and reading the private investigator reports had been emotional for him, and Brianna had been there to help him through it.

"When?"

He glanced down at the woman he held in his arms. "When what, sweetheart?"

"When did you know you loved me?"

He smiled. "I honestly think it was when I arrived in town and saw you with that ice-cream cone. I thought about you the rest of the day and night, and then to see you again at the reading of Ellen's will was mind-blowing. All I knew was that I wanted to see you again, which was why I rushed back to Wyoming on Thursday. I finally accepted I loved you when you whispered the words to me, but I should have known based on how I felt when you asked for my sperm."

She covered her face. "I can't believe I asked you that."

"As you can see from our sexual encounters, I am all in." He uncovered her face with his hands and said, "Now tell me when you fell in love with me."

She smiled up at him. "It was the summer after my first year at college."

"But we hadn't even met," he said.

"I know. It was the first summer I returned home from college after my breakup with Alan. I hung around the ranch, too embarrassed to go into town. Ms. Ellen got me to organize the attic to keep me busy. That's when I came across that PI report with your college graduation picture."

She shifted in his lap and wrapped her arms around his neck. "I saw it, thought you were quite a handsome young man and decided to make you my fantasy boyfriend."

He chuckled. "Your fantasy boyfriend?"

"Yes. The more I thought about you, the less I thought about Alan and the pain he had caused me. Needless to say, that summer I got all into you, Cashen Outlaw. Then when I saw you that day at the reading of the will, I knew you could be my fantasy everything. I realized I loved you when I was trying to make up my mind about your counterproposal. I decided that if you never fell in love with me, I would love you anyway, and I would love the baby you would give me."

"Um, the baby I *have* given you," he said, touching her stomach. "I have a feeling you got pregnant during our honeymoon."

A huge smile spread across her face. "I have that same feeling. I hope so."

"I hope so, too. And what we have has nothing to do with the land, Brianna. It's about me loving you, you loving me and us wanting a baby together. It's all about love."

And then he lowered his mouth to hers.

* * *

Bart Outlaw walked into his study at the Outlaw Estates in Fairbanks after being told by his housekeeper that his son Cash wanted to see him. He saw Cash with some woman and wondered what this was about.

"What's going on, Cash?"

Cash turned to his father. "First, I'd like you to meet my wife."

"Wife?"

"Yes, I got married last Wednesday. This is Brianna Banks Outlaw. Brianna, this is my father, Bart. Now, with that out of the way, I want to know why you had your attorneys send Brianna a letter saying I was contesting my mother's will?"

"Because you should have contested it! And why did you feel the need to marry her?" an angry Bart asked. "I had things under control. You would have gotten everything."

"As usual, you stuck your nose where it didn't belong, Dad. I told you from the beginning I thought Ellen did the right thing in her will. And to set the record straight, the reason I married Brianna had nothing to do with the land. It had to do with me falling in love with her. And what about all those times you refused to let Ellen reach out to me while I was growing up? Who gave you the right?"

"It was a decision I made as your father. Had she really wanted you she would have gotten you."

"She tried. I know she took you to court to get custody of me."

"And she lost. I had to teach her a lesson about

what can happen when anyone tries to go against Bart Outlaw."

Cash didn't say anything. At that moment he knew his father didn't regret anything he'd done because he felt he was justified.

"I'm moving to Wyoming," Cash said.

"You're what!"

"You heard me. I am moving to Wyoming."

He saw the color actually drain from Bart's features. "You're leaving the company?" Bart asked in a shocked voice.

A part of Cash wished he could say yes, he was leaving the company, knowing how much such a thing would hurt the old man. Instead he said, "No, I will still be working for the company, but not here. Now more than ever I need to get away from here. Get away from you. Hopefully, one day you will realize what a huge mistake you made in trying to control my life. Goodbye, Dad."

And without saying anything else, Cash took Brianna's hand and walked out of the house.

Epilogue

A month later

It was a beautiful day for a wedding celebration in honor of Cash and Brianna Outlaw. The affair was hosted on the grounds of the Blazing Frontier Ranch. Family, friends and plenty of townsfolk were in attendance to celebrate the affair.

The couple walked around greeting their guests. Brianna got the chance to introduce Cash to a lot of the locals he hadn't yet met. Everyone was happy to welcome him to town, especially after hearing the announcement that he would be reopening the dude ranch. They knew that would be a big boost for the economy.

Brianna met the members of Cash's family that she hadn't yet met, including his sister, Charm. She and

Charm became friends immediately. She also met those other Westmorelands, including motorcycle legend Thorn Westmoreland, and bestselling author Rock Mason (aka Stone Westmoreland).

The announcement that the ranch would also be a horse ranch was met with loud cheers. There was another announcement, too. However, it was one Brianna and Cash wanted to keep between themselves for a while. They were expecting their first child. She had indeed gotten pregnant during their honeymoon.

The happy couple were talking to Garth and Regan when Garth glanced over Cash's shoulder and said, "Look who's here."

Cash turned and saw his father had arrived with Claudia. Although Bart had called weeks ago and apologized to Cash and Brianna for what he had done, Cash hadn't known whether or not he would come to the wedding celebration.

Since Claudia was with Bart, Cash had a feeling she was responsible for both the apology and Bart's appearance today. They had heard from Charm that Claudia had raked Bart over the coals after hearing about what he had done to Cash, in the past and the present.

Cash and Brianna had accepted Bart's apology. They just wanted to look to the future and not dwell on the past. Cash was looking forward to a long and peaceful life with his wife and family at their ranch home in Wyoming.

Cash and his brothers knew they needed to have a heart-to-heart talk with their father about a lot of things. It was time he leveled with them about why he still felt the need to run their lives and why he still could not accept the Westmorelands as their kin, when it was obvious that they were.

That talk would not take place today. Today was Cash and Brianna's time to celebrate their marriage. As Cash gazed down at his wife, he was glad the marriage he'd demanded had landed Brianna right where he wanted her to be, a permanent part of his life.

* * * * *

Look for Sloan's story,
available December 2021!

When the woman responsible for Sloan Outlaw's
one and only heartbreak needs help,
Sloan can't refuse.
Sure, he'll help her save her company,
but the one thing he wants out of the deal is her.

WE HOPE YOU ENJOYED
THIS BOOK FROM

HARLEQUIN
DESIRE

*Luxury, scandal, desire—welcome to
the lives of the American elite.*

Be transported to the worlds of oil barons, family dynasties,
moguls and celebrities. Get ready for juicy plot twists,
delicious sensuality and intriguing scandal.

6 NEW BOOKS AVAILABLE EVERY MONTH!

COMING NEXT MONTH FROM

DESIRE

Available May 11, 2021

#2803 THE TROUBLE WITH BAD BOYS
Texas Cattleman's Club: Heir Apparent
by Katherine Garbera
Landing bad boy influencer Zach Benning to promote Royal's biggest
soiree is a highlight for hardworking Lila Jones. And the event's marketing
isn't all that's made over! Lila's sexy new look sets their relationship on
fire... Will it burn hot enough to last?

#2804 SECOND CHANCE COUNTRY
Dynasties: Beaumont Bay • by Jessica Lemmon
Country music star Cash Sutherland hasn't seen Presley Cole since he
broke her heart. Now a journalist, she's back in his life and determined to
get answers he doesn't want to give. Will their renewed passion distract
her from the truth?

#2805 SEDUCTION, SOUTHERN STYLE
Sweet Tea and Scandal • by Cat Schield
When Sienna Burns gets close to CEO Ethan Watts to help her adopted
sister, she's disarmed by his Southern charm, sex appeal...and insistence
on questioning her intentions. Now their explosive chemistry has created
divided loyalties that may derail all her plans...

#2806 THE LAST LITTLE SECRET
Sin City Secrets • by Zuri Day
It's strictly business when real estate developer Nick Breedlove hires
interior designer—and former lover—Samantha Price for his new project.
Sparks fly again, but Samantha is hiding a secret. And when he learns the
truth about her son, she may lose him forever...

#2807 THE REBEL HEIR
by Niobia Bryant
Handsome restaurant heir Coleman Cress has always been rebellious—
in business and in relationships. Sharing a secret no-strings affair with
confident Cress family chef Jillian Rossi is no different. But when lust
becomes something more, can their relationship survive meddling exes
and family drama?

#2808 HOLLYWOOD EX FACTOR
LA Women • by Sheri WhiteFeather
Security specialist Zeke Mitchell was never interested in the spotlight.
When his wife, Margot Jensen, returns to acting, their marriage ends...but
the attraction doesn't. As things heat up, are the problems of their past too
big to overlook?

HDCNM0421

SPECIAL EXCERPT FROM

⟨H⟩ HARLEQUIN

DESIRE

*Country music star Cash Sutherland hasn't seen
Presley Cole since he broke her heart. Now a journalist,
she's back in his life and determined to get answers he
doesn't want to give. Will their renewed passion distract
her from the truth?*

Read on for a sneak peek at
Second Chance Love Song
by Jessica Lemmon.

"Did you expect me to sleep in here with you?"

And there it was. The line that he hadn't thought to draw
but now was obvious he'd need to draw.

He eased back on the bed, shoved a pillow behind his
back and curled her into his side. Arranging the blankets
over both of them, he leaned over and kissed her wild hair,
smiling against it when he thought about the tangles she'd
have to comb out later. He hoped she thought of why they
were there when she did.

"We should talk about that, yeah?" he asked rhetorically.
He felt her stiffen in his arms. "I want you here, Pres. In this
bed. Naked in my arms. I want you on my dock, driving me
wild in that tiny pink bikini. But we should be clear about
what this is…and what it's not."

She shifted and looked up at him, her blue eyes wide and
innocent, her lips pursed gently. "What it's not."

"Yeah, honey," he continued, gentler than before. "What
it's not."

"You mean…" She licked those pink lips and rested a hand tenderly on his chest. "You mean you aren't going to marry me and make an honest woman out of me after that?"

Cash's face broadcasted myriad emotions. From what Presley could see, they ranged from regret to nervousness to confusion and finally to what she could only describe as "oh, shit." That was when she decided to let him off the hook.

Chuckling, she shoved away from him, still holding the sheet to her chest. "God, your face! I'm kidding. Cash, honestly."

He blinked, held that confused expression a few moments longer and then gave her a very unsure half smile. "I knew that."

"I'm not the girl you left at Florida State," she told him. "I grew up, too, you know. I learned how the world worked. I experienced life beyond the bubble I lived in."

She took his hand and laced their fingers together. She still cared about him, so much. After that, she cared more than before. But she also wasn't so foolish to believe that sex—even earth-shattering sex—had the power to change the past. The past was him promising to wait for her and then leaving and never looking back.

"That was really fun," she continued. "I had a great time. You looked like you had a great time. I'm looking forward to doing it again if you're up to the task."

Don't miss what happens next in…
Second Chance Love Song
by Jessica Lemmon, the second book in the
Dynasties: Beaumont Bay series!

Available May 2021 wherever
Harlequin Desire books and ebooks are sold.

Harlequin.com

Get 4 FREE REWARDS!

We'll send you 2 FREE Books plus 2 FREE Mystery Gifts.

Harlequin Desire books transport you to the world of the American elite with juicy plot twists, delicious sensuality and intriguing scandal.

FREE Value Over **$20**

YES! Please send me 2 FREE Harlequin Desire novels and my 2 FREE gifts (gifts are worth about $10 retail). After receiving them, if I don't wish to receive any more books, I can return the shipping statement marked "cancel." If I don't cancel, I will receive 6 brand-new novels every month and be billed just $4.55 per book in the U.S. or $5.24 per book in Canada. That's a savings of at least 13% off the cover price! It's quite a bargain! Shipping and handling is just 50¢ per book in the U.S. and $1.25 per book in Canada.* I understand that accepting the 2 free books and gifts places me under no obligation to buy anything. I can always return a shipment and cancel at any time. The free books and gifts are mine to keep no matter what I decide.

225/326 HDN GNND

Name (please print)

Address   Apt. #

City   State/Province   Zip/Postal Code

Email: Please check this box ☐ if you would like to receive newsletters and promotional emails from Harlequin Enterprises ULC and its affiliates. You can unsubscribe anytime.

> ### Mail to the **Harlequin Reader Service:**
> **IN U.S.A.:** P.O. Box 1341, Buffalo, NY 14240-8531
> **IN CANADA:** P.O. Box 603, Fort Erie, Ontario L2A 5X3

Want to try 2 free books from another series? Call 1-800-873-8635 or visit www.ReaderService.com.

---

*Terms and prices subject to change without notice. Prices do not include sales taxes, which will be charged (if applicable) based on your state or country of residence. Canadian residents will be charged applicable taxes. Offer not valid in Quebec. This offer is limited to one order per household. Books received may not be as shown. Not valid for current subscribers to Harlequin Desire books. All orders subject to approval. Credit or debit balances in a customer's account(s) may be offset by any other outstanding balance owed by or to the customer. Please allow 4 to 6 weeks for delivery. Offer available while quantities last.

Your Privacy—Your information is being collected by Harlequin Enterprises ULC, operating as Harlequin Reader Service. For a complete summary of the information we collect, how we use this information and to whom it is disclosed, please visit our privacy notice located at corporate.harlequin.com/privacy-notice. From time to time we may also exchange your personal information with reputable third parties. If you wish to opt out of this sharing of your personal information, please visit readerservice.com/consumerschoice or call 1-800-873-8635. **Notice to California Residents**—Under California law, you have specific rights to control and access your data. For more information on these rights and how to exercise them, visit corporate.harlequin.com/california-privacy.

HD21R